HIT & RUN

HIT & RUN

A Delilah West Thriller

MAXINE O'CALLAGHAN

BRASH
BOOKS

Text copyright © 1989, 2015 Maxine O'Callaghan
All rights reserved.
Printed in the United States of America.
No part of this book may be reproduced, or stored in a retrieval system, or transmitted in any form or by any means, electronic, mechanical, photocopying, recording, or otherwise, without express written permission of the publisher.

Library of Congress Cataloging-in-Publication Data

O'Callaghan, Maxine.
Hit and run.
I. Title.

PS3565.C35H5 1989   813'.54   88–30812

ISBN: 1941298621
ISBN-13: 9781941298626

Published by Brash Books, LLC
12120 State Line, #253
Leawood, Kansas 66209

www.brash-books.com

For my mother, Daisy Brelland,
who gave me a special gift—my love of
the written word.

Several people helped with the preparation of this
book. Martha Molodowitch and Karen Cate typed
the original manuscript onto computer disk.
Fred O'Callaghan coordinated everything and
helped me keep a tight schedule. I thank them.

And a special thanks to my agent, Jane Jordan Browne, for
her good advice, encouragement, and incredible tenacity.

ONE

I began to shiver when the paramedics put the old man on a stretcher and covered up his face. The damp January chill had turned to an icy drizzle, quickly soaking through my sweats. Beautiful southern California.

Besides the rescue van, there was a fire engine on the scene plus an ambulance, two Santa Ana patrol cars, a crime lab unit, and an unmarked car with official plates. Flashing lights strobed the wet pavement, and static-filled communications crackled eerily through the air.

A fireman draped a slicker over my shoulders and said, "Better have that knee taken care of." He led me over to the paramedics.

I watched the stretcher being loaded into the ambulance while a medic swabbed the scrape on my knee.

"We'll take you in and let ER get an X ray," he said.

"No, thanks. I'm okay."

My main concern was to make sure the police got the bastard who clipped me and left an old man dead in the rain-slick street. I'd given them a good description when I called in. A black Trans Am with gold flames painted along the front fenders and three letters that made up half the license plate.

Digging my hands into the pockets of the oversized slicker and drawing it tight, I limped over to the group clustered around the spot in the gutter where the old man had lain. A photographer snapped pictures. The first patrolman to arrive on the scene finished his report to a bulky man who hunched his head, turtlelike, into the turned-up collar of a beige raincoat and looked as miserable as I felt.

"Lieutenant Brady, this is the witness. Miss—" The patrolman peered at his notebook and said, "West?"

"Delilah West." I looked down at the empty spot on the asphalt that was illuminated in harsh flashes of the camera's strobe. "Who was he? I didn't check his identification."

"Name was Joseph Collins," Brady said. "Seventy-two years old. He lived over on the other side of the park in a retirement hotel. Can't figure what the hell he was doing out wandering around this time of night." Brady had a balding head and a walrus mustache beaded with moisture. There was cautious friendliness in his businesslike tone. "Understand you're a P.I., Miss West. Break for us having a professional as a witness."

"Did you find the car?"

"Not the last I heard." Brady turned to the patrolman. "Check it out, will you?" As the officer walked away, Brady turned back to me. "How's the leg? You up to giving me a statement?"

"I'm fine," I said. "But, listen, there's something I have to tell you. This is not the spot where I found the—where I found Mr. Collins."

Both Brady and the photographer stared at me.

"You moved the body?" Brady asked, incredulous.

"At that point, Mr. Collins was not a body," I said. "It seemed like a good idea to get him out of the street while I called for help."

"Christ," Brady muttered. "All right, Miss West. Let's hear it from the beginning. Any more interesting details you forgot to mention?"

So much for professional rapport. He pulled his head back farther into the carapace of his trench coat and stayed right on my heels, while I led him to the middle of the street. The rain came down harder, driven by the wind.

I told Brady that I had been out jogging. Nobody questioned exercise even on a godawful night like that, so I didn't have to explain that I had no apartment to go to and I was bored and restless camped out in my office. I'd been minding my own business, leaning against a lamppost and gasping for breath, when the Trans Am slid around the corner and the rear end cut loose.

With a ton of metal climbing the curb and sliding in my direction, there was not a whole lot of time for graceful retreat. I dived off in the opposite direction, ending up in a bruising roll, pain flaring through my leg as my knee hit cement.

The only reason I got a look at the car was that the sidewalk was slippery with leaves and mud, so it took a few seconds for the driver to regain control before he roared off in the darkness.

"You see Collins before the car ran him down?" Brady asked.

I shook my head. "No, but I'd just come around the corner and then everything happened too fast."

As a matter of fact, I didn't even notice the old man lying there right away. I'd heard a thud mixed in with the howl of tires and screech of brakes, but the noise hadn't really registered. I was hobbling toward a phone booth down at the end of the block, wondering whom to call for a ride, when I saw what looked like a lumpy pile of old clothes in the middle of the street. That soft, meaty thump— suddenly I remembered it as I rushed out, the sound vivid and distinct as though I'd fed the memory into a computer and enhanced it.

He was lying on his stomach, one arm beneath him, the other flung outward, thin white hair blowing across his skull, blood trickling from his mouth. No pulse, but I wasn't willing to pronounce him dead. And I couldn't leave him there in the street while I went to call for help. Broken bones were probably the least of his injuries, but I ran my hands quickly over his body and down his legs. One shoe was missing, and his foot felt small, delicate beneath a wet sock.

He wore a tan raincoat. Working gently, I turned him over, straddled his legs, grasped the coat on either side of his body, and pulled toward the curb. An easy job. He was a fragile bundle of light bones and spare flesh. I had tucked the coat back around him before I left.

At the time, I was sure I had no other choice, but now I wondered if my precautions had been only wishful thinking.

Brady's temper got shorter, and his voice got louder as he questioned me. He made me repeat every detail at least two times more than was necessary, just to make sure I knew he considered me a rank amateur and a bumbling idiot.

The photographer kept taking pictures, but, in the darkness, there wasn't a lot to see, and the rain sluiced away tire marks and debris and the old man's blood. The only thing that turned up was Collins's missing shoe. The patrolman discovered it in the gutter on the opposite side of the street, and we all trooped over.

As Brady bagged the glistening, well-polished leather, something niggled at the back of my mind, but I was too wiped out to pursue it. Fortunately Brady was exhausted too. He grudgingly okayed a ride for me with the patrolman, adding "I'll want you at the station first thing tomorrow to sign a statement, Miss West."

As we got into the black and white, the patrolman said, "Where to?"

Good question.

What I needed was a nice hot bath, but there was nobody I wanted to impose on in the middle of the night. So I told him I'd left my car at the office and asked to be dropped off there.

By the time we arrived, there was still no word about the Trans Am. The way my luck was running the guy who'd mowed down me and Joseph Collins was long gone.

Dammit, Christmas was over and the cute little kid in the diaper was supposed to wipe the slate clean and give everybody a fresh start. While I took a spit bath in the ladies' room and crawled into a sleeping bag beside my desk, I brooded about the past eleven months and wondered if history was getting together a repeat performance.

It was a very bad year.

In February I had spent two weeks tracking down the wife of a distraught man who told me she suffered from recurring bouts of amnesia. "When you find her, don't scare her," he said. "Just call and I'll come right away." Well, I did and he did. He showed up promptly with a .357 Magnum and blasted her all over room 426 of the Thrifty Nifty Motel.

The state threatened to pull my license. The county threatened to charge me with Accessory to Murder One. The Thrifty Nifty Motel threatened to sue…until they got a look at my assets.

In April I served a subpoena to a dope dealer who did sumo wrestling on the side. He shoved back the paper with a straight-arm delivery that catapulted me over the stoop, broke my arm, cracked two ribs, and opened up my thigh to the tune of twenty-three stitches.

In May I discovered that medical insurance is only for healthy people and nobody loves a loser. I was declared a bad risk, and my policy was canceled.

In June my car died.

In August I had to choose between paying the rent on my apartment or my office.

In October…well, you get the picture.

By December I was moonlighting, waiting tables at Mom's Kountry Kooking in Santa Ana. At least I got one free meal a day and the tips were good. Anyway, things are always slow in the P.I. business during the holidays. People still disappear, fool around with their secretaries and/or bosses, steal their kids, embezzle, and shoot dope. But hope, that eternal bamboozler, fools the ones who are robbed and cheated into thinking that maybe, somehow, Virginia, there is a Santy Claus who's going to whip up a miracle for them.

Come January—well, I had hopes because January is usually my best month. Until then I could scrape by on the job at Mom's and a weekly poker game with the kitchen help. We were an eclectic group: Latino, Salvadorian, Hmong, and me, the token female WASP. A little language problem, but no matter. We all understood five card draw, deuces wild, jacks or better to open.

Some days I thought it would be easy to forget the detective trade. No stakeouts. No sleazeballs stiffing you out of your fee.

Then a customer would call me sweet thing and pinch my fanny. Oh, yes. Waitressing was a real career move.

On December 4, a little more than a month ago, the temperature hit ninety degrees two days in a row. Christmas shoppers grumbled about having to buy presents when they could be working on their tan. Mom's was well into the lunch crush when the hostess steered a familiar squat figure over to my station.

"Hello, Charlie." I slapped down silverware, a napkin, a glass of ice water.

"Delilah?" He stared up at me, frog-faced. "What are you doing here?"

"Serving lunch. The special's a tuna sandwich with a side of stuffing." Everything at Mom's came with a side of stuffing.

"I suppose it's an employee thing." He glanced around and lowered his voice. "What is it? Theft?"

"No, survival. I like to eat and pay my bills."

"You closed your agency?"

"No, it's surviving too. How about some coffee?"

He fiddled with his silverware while I brought his drink and the salad he ordered, avoiding my eyes. Embarrassed by my circumstances. Well, I wasn't. Slinging hash is good, honest work, just a little hard on the ankles.

Charlie Colfax looked prosperous, as always. Expensive threads, Italian shoes, a Rolex under his immaculate cuff. The Colfax Agency was the biggest in Orange County, the third largest in California. Five years ago when my husband, Jack, died, Charlie offered me a job. He and Jack had been partners once, a long time ago. I had the feeling he owed Jack, old debts that Charlie never talked about. Instead, he renewed his job offer regularly, even though I kept turning him down.

Now as I schlepped hamburgers and taco salads, I thought about a regular salary, regular hours. Pensions, bonuses, paid vacations.

He left me a 12 percent tip and a note on his business card to call him first thing the next morning. By then I'd had time to think about the eight-to-five, cog-in-the-wheel grind.

"You finally ready to give up on your one-man show?" Charlie demanded.

I also remembered that it was only a month until January and things were bound to pick up. "Not just yet, Charlie, but thanks anyway."

"Figures. Well, tell you what. I'm understaffed right now and I do have something I could farm out if you're interested."

At that point I thought, of course, that my run of bad luck was over.

My assignment was store detective at May Company at South Coast Plaza. Looking for shoplifters isn't my favorite thing to do and it's as hard on the feet as waiting tables, but I wasn't complaining. After the second week, I was even thinking, as I mingled with the crowds in Ladies Accessories, about looking for a new apartment. That's when I spotted the woman tucking eighteen-carat earrings into an oversized handbag.

She was the perfect silver-haired, sweet-faced old granny, the one who sells you cookies and long-distance telephone calls on TV. So much for stereotypes. I tracked her through Leather Goods, Ladies Wear, and the perfume counter, right behind her as she left the store with her bulging bag.

"Excuse me, ma'am," I said, pleasant but firm.

She turned, froze, blinked, then began yelling her head off. Two upstanding fellows in Hawaiian shirts came to her rescue, body-blocking me just long enough so she could get a head start.

I shoved my way free and ran after her. More helpful citizens pitched in, getting in the way, yelling threats. Then one stuck out his foot and I went sprawling, crashing into a planter.

"If you were a regular employee, you'd have insurance and disability," Charlie said when I called to tell him my foot was swollen to twice its normal size. Then he had given me two hundred dollars and some advice: "Consider another line of work."

Now, a month later, as I tried to get comfortable on my office floor, I wondered if Charlie was right. Fate had been bashing me over the head with some regularity for a whole year, and I had the scars to prove it. Boy, did I have the scars.

My knee throbbed and I ached in a dozen new and unrelated places. Every time I closed my eyes I saw the black Trans Am hurtling straight at me.

This had to be it. Nadir. Bottom of the barrel. Things couldn't possibly get worse.

But, of course, they always do.

TWO

The next morning I went to eat breakfast at Mom's and angle to get my job back until I could decide on a new career. Brain surgeon? Nuclear physicist?

Jorge Sanchez waved from the kitchen. Hoa Phuoc finished bussing a table and brought me a discarded newspaper.

"Thanks," I said.

"*De nada.*" A shy, sad smile.

He wasn't so hot at English, but he was picking up Spanish fast.

I bit into my bagel, opened the paper, and discovered that the hit and run was front-page news. Two pictures went along with the article, one of Joseph Collins, "longtime resident and well-known businessman," the other of the Trans Am's driver.

Michael Morales, age nineteen, was a skinny kid with bad skin and scraggly hair. Morales had a record of juvenile arrests. Unspecified, naturally, since juvenile records are protected by the courts. He was charged with felony hit and run.

Thanks to me, this time he was playing with the grown-ups. Maybe my luck was changing after all.

Then I turned the page and read about the funeral arrangements for Joseph Collins. Retribution was all very well, but the old man was still dead, mourned by a daughter, Pamela Jacobs, a son-in-law, Kenneth, and a granddaughter, Carolyn. There was nothing about why he was out alone so late at night. Was he senile? An insomniac?

I got a little free advertising in a sidebar under the headline: *Concerned Citizens Do Make a Difference.* They even spelled my name right.

I finished my coffee, waved good-bye to Jorge, and headed off to the Santa Ana police station. Brady was a bit more civil this morning due to the quick arrest of Morales and the good press. After only the standard amount of delays and confusion, I signed my statement and escaped.

By then the rush hour was over. As I returned to my office, the rain settled into a sullen, fitful drizzle. I realized that I'd forgotten all about asking for my job back at Mom's. I could change course and go back, but there was always the possibility that Hollywood had called while I was out, wanting to buy my life story.

The building that houses my one-room office is a basic stucco box, three stories high, located within brisk walking distance of the Civic Center, Orange County's central judicial and governmental complex. It was built in the early sixties for a quick profit and left to deteriorate like the rest of the neighborhood. I pulled into a No Parking space next to a dumpster and went in the back way.

Over the years, a stream of maintenance men have struggled with the grimy floors, inadequate plumbing, and faulty wiring. As the building gets older, the janitors seem to get scrawnier and seedier. The latest is a dried-up little man named Harry Polk. He has short gray hair that looks as if he cuts it with a pocket knife, and he always dresses in a dingy white T-shirt and corduroy pants the color of used motor oil.

When I came in, he was passing a desultory mop over the tiled area in front of the stairs. He looked up, saw me, and rushed over, mop in hand, trailing dribbles of dirty water.

"Miz West, you okay?" His gray eyes bulged with excitement. "That was really something, you catching that Morales guy. But I'll betcha the paper didn't tell the half of it. Did he pull a knife? Did you have to use karate?"

Poor Harry. I've been a big disappointment to him, and today I'd be batting a thousand. When he took the janitor's job two months ago, the discovery of an honest-to-God private eye in the building really brightened up his life. The fact that I was a woman didn't bother him, but it did bring out his protective instincts. He lurked in corridors to scrutinize my few visitors, and when they left, he followed them to their cars. "Just in case," he'd say darkly and hand me greasy scraps of paper with license numbers and strangely abbreviated descriptions penciled in shaky script. Harry knew that I was living in the office, but I pretended to work late, and he pretended to believe me.

Feeling a bit guilty that I couldn't produce a shootout or at least a high-speed car chase, I said, "The paper was right, Harry. All I did was give the police a description of the hit-and-run car."

"Oh." His narrow shoulders sagged, but, as I headed for the stairs, he perked up and said, "Geez, I almost forgot. There's this woman hanging around your office, Miz West. She came in about an hour ago. Told her I didn't know when you'd be back, but she'd said she'd wait around just in case you showed up."

If she wasn't from Hollywood, maybe she was a real, live client.

Harry fumbled in his pocket and handed me an old envelope covered with scribbles. "She's about five foot two, hundred and forty pounds, reddish hair, forty-five years old. It's all there. Oh, and she don't drive a car, but I saw her get off the bus, so I wrote down the number. I don't much like the looks of her, Miz West. If you want, I can come up with you and—"

"That's all right, Harry. If I need you, I'll signal."

"I'll be right here," he promised. "Just bang on the register like I told you."

Harry had discovered that sound resonated through the heating ducts and was clearly audible in the lobby. Two long and two short raps, and he'd be up quick as a flash, he told me, pipe wrench in hand.

The woman Harry worried about leaned against the wall beside my office door, a resigned look on her puffy face. I had a feeling life always left her waiting around in dark corridors.

She looked up hopefully as I came down the hall. Harry's estimations of weight, height, and age were on the mark. She wore a raincoat, buttoned and belted around her pudgy body. The coat looked new, a soft mauve color in a suedelike fabric, and contrasted sharply with her scuffed oxfords and cracked vinyl handbag.

I took out my key and said, "I understand you're waiting for me. I'm Delilah West."

She straightened, screwing up her courage. "I'm sorry I don't have an appointment, but I gotta talk to you. It's really important."

"All right. Come on in."

I unlocked the door, let her go ahead of me, and switched on the lights. I'd stowed my sleeping bag and personal things in the closet and the room looked surprisingly cheerful. Besides the usual desk, file cabinets, and side chair, I'd brought in a comfortable wingback from my apartment furniture. Beside it, an oak table held a brass lamp with a nubby fabric shade and an exuberantly healthy philodendron in a large red clay pot, thriving on leftover coffee and neglect.

I offered her the side chair. "Sit down, won't you, Mrs...."

"Simpson, Arlene Simpson." She perched on the edge and followed me with anxious eyes as I walked around my desk and stopped to switch on the hotplate that sat on top of a file cabinet.

"How about some coffee?" I picked up the teakettle, decided it contained enough water for two, and set it down again. I wanted to put the woman at ease, but she shook her head, her face tight with tension. I tried again. "Can I take your coat? It's a bit stuffy in here."

"No. Well..." She fingered the buttons, then slowly undid them, slid her arms from the sleeves, but kept the coat draped over her shoulders. Beneath it she wore a pink uniform with "Arlene" stitched in red on a pocket over her left breast. I knew the look well, having worn a little number just like it at Mom's.

"I took off from work to come and see you," she explained. "I have to go back for the lunch shift. I work over at Al's Place. Maybe you know it. Just off the freeway on Seventeenth?"

I shook my head, and she plunged on, the floodgates finally open.

"Well, I'm not surprised. It's pretty small, but we got good coffee, and a lot of truckers stop in. And Al—he's really nice to me. He let me come over here and after lunch I hafta take off to go over to the courthouse and…" She trailed off as if she'd run out of air, gulped a deep breath, and went on. "I guess I'd better ask you one thing, Miss West. What do you—I mean, how much does it cost to have you investigate something?"

"My standard fee is forty dollars an hour, plus expenses."

She looked as though I'd slapped her. "So much…I didn't think—look, I don't have the money right now, but could I pay you something every week? Sort of like on time? With interest—I'd be glad to pay interest."

Lord, I thought, watching her red-knuckled hands knead her handbag. What was the old warning: Be careful what you wish for… Well, a client is a client, even on the easy payment plan.

"Maybe we can work something out," I said. "Why don't you just tell me what's wrong, Mrs. Simpson?"

"It's my son. He's in terrible trouble. They put him in jail. The police say he killed somebody."

"Maybe I should explain something," I said gently. "I'm not authorized to investigate murders, so I don't know how much I can do for your son. You'd be better off spending your money on a good attorney."

"He has a lawyer, a Mr. Scott. The judge appointed him. But it doesn't make any difference. There's only one person who can help us, and that's you, Miss West."

The only one who could help? I didn't know what she'd heard about me, but maybe I ought to give her my record for the past year.

"Please, Miss West," she said.

"Well, all right." What could it hurt to listen? "Why don't you start from the beginning?"

"First, I guess I'd better tell you who my son is." Her grip tightened on her handbag. She hugged it to her breast like a shield.

I've never thought I was psychic or had ESP, but—hoo boy—I did know something was coming.

"My son's name," she said, "is Michael Morales."

THREE

Michael Morales.

I stared at her, remembering the sullen, defiant face in the newspaper picture.

The teakettle whistled, so I got up and turned off the burner, picked up a couple of mugs and shook in some Maxim, glad to have something to do except sit there with my mouth hanging open. All her talk of wanting to hire me—was this really a pay-as-you-go bribe to get me to change my story? I took the mug back to the desk and sat down.

Her chin trembled. "I said it wrong." Tears spilled down her cheeks, and she fumbled for a tissue. "Oh, God, I've made a mess of things and I don't—I can't—" She hunched over and wept, in quiet, racking sobs.

Michael Morales killed that old man, I reminded myself. Of course she was upset, but that didn't alter the fact that her son ran Mr. Collins down and left him in the street.

I opened my bottom desk drawer and took out a bottle of brandy. I added a generous dollop to her coffee, and put the my in front of her.

"Drink that," I said.

She didn't argue. She drank, shuddering.

"More?"

She shook her head and wiped her eyes, blew her nose. "I'm sorry. I didn't mean to break down like that. It's just—it's been so awful—a nightmare—and then I thought if I came here—"

"Frankly, I don't know why you did." I wrapped my hands around the mug, warming them briefly before I took a swallow. "This is damned awkward, Mrs. Simpson. I'm an eyewitness to a hit and run involving your son. I really don't think I can talk to you about it."

"Please, if you'll just let me explain…I know you think you saw Mike—"

"Mrs. Simpson, your son almost ran over me too."

"He told me. He was going a little too fast and the car went into a skid. It was *raining*. He saw you jump out of the way, and he should of stopped. He knows that now. But he panicked."

"No," I said. "He panicked when he hit Mr. Collins."

She shook her head. "That old man—no, Mike never saw him. He didn't know a thing about it till the police took him down and booked him. He thought they arrested him because of you."

So that's the way he's going to play it, I thought.

"Mike's not a bad kid," she went on. "He's been in a little trouble, but that's because it was awfully hard for him after his dad died. For me too. We were all so close."

Her story happened all the time. A single mother, no family, being forced to take an unskilled job and move to the edge of the barrio, trouble with her son. "The school—well, it was really bad, and poor Mike—the white kids used to call him Frijole Face, stuff like that. And the Mexican kids, to them he was just another Anglo."

By the time Michael entered high school, he was in with a bad crowd and had some minor brushes with the law. And his mother's second marriage was breaking up. "That was a terrible time for me, Mrs. West. I wasn't paying enough attention to Mike, so he got out of hand. All my fault. But Mike's been getting his head straight, really he is. He's got a job in a service station. He's really a good mechanic. He fixed up that car himself. And we had such a nice Christmas. He bought me this coat." She fingered the velvety fabric, and her face softened. "He didn't do it, Miss West. He didn't kill that old man. There's been a terrible mistake."

I sighed and drank some more coffee. It was lukewarm but potent. "Mrs. Simpson, I feel sorry for you. Maybe I even feel a little sorry for your son. If coming here and talking about it makes you feel better, fine. But if you really think he didn't kill Mr. Collins, you'd better go find another investigator to try and prove it. I can't help you."

"But that's just it. You're the only one who can." She was a mother defending her child, and she forgot to be nervous. "Don't you have one little doubt about what you saw? It must've been over awfully fast, and it was so dark. Did you actually see Mike run that old man down?"

"Well—no," I admitted. "But I know what happened."

"But if you didn't see it—"

"I heard it," I said.

"What? What did you hear?"

"A kind of thump. The sound of the car striking flesh."

She flinched, but said stubbornly, "Maybe it was something else. It'd been windy. There was all kinds of stuff blown into the streets."

"There's probably other evidence." I hadn't asked Brady about physical evidence, but it was likely there was some.

"But you don't know for sure, do you?"

"Look, even if it's possible I made a mistake—"

She leaned forward eagerly.

"—I said *if*, and if your son didn't hit Mr. Collins, who did?"

"That's why I want to hire you, Miss West. I want you to find out exactly what happened. When you do, you'll convince yourself that Mike's telling the truth. I know you will."

It made a weird kind of sense, but I didn't want any part of it. In the first place, I couldn't take money from the woman. It might be illegal. It was certainly unethical.

"I'm sorry," I said. "I can't do it."

"Will you at least think about it?"

"Mrs. Simpson—"

"Please," she said like a prayer. "Please."

"All right, I'll think about it. But I'm not promising anything," I warned.

After Arlene Simpson left, I prowled the office, stopping to stare out the window into early darkness. Thick clouds canceled out the twilight. I shivered and turned away. God, how I hate rainy January nights. I went back to my desk and took a sip of coffee, but it was cold so I poured it into the flowerpot.

"Did you actually see Mike run that old man down?"

I hadn't. So what? I don't see the sun go around the world, but when it comes up in the morning, I've got a pretty good idea where it's been.

Catchy comparison—did it really apply?

"Did you actually see Mike run that old man down?"

No, but—but what? Mr. Collins was dead, and I had heard *something*. I tried to remember the sequence of sounds exactly: the engine as the car raced down Arbor, a kind of bump-bump, then the howl of tires.

It felt wrong, somehow, but I couldn't figure out why. Was it possible that somebody else had hit Mr. Collins before Mike came along? There was no way I could know that. I'd only just come around the corner on Arbor. So—yes. A possibility.

I went through it again, and this time the whole night unreeled: my fall and the Trans Am speeding away, finding the old man. Dragging him to the curb and waiting for the paramedics. The long session with Lieutenant Brady. Everything, down to the rain glistening on Mr. Collins's polished shoe.

A quick double knock interrupted my thoughts. Harry opened the door to poke his head inside.

"You all right, Miz West? I saw that woman leave in a big hurry. She's headed for the bus stop. I got an hour for lunch. You want me to follow her?"

"No, Harry. But thanks anyway."

"Oh, okay." He left, disappointed.

The phone rang. It was Rita. Rita Braddock runs the service that fields my calls. An answering machine would be cheaper, but I owe her too much money to drop her service. Anyway, we've been friends for years so I know she won't turn my account over to a collection agency—at least for a while yet.

"Jeez, I guess you really are desperate," she said. "Throwing yourself under cars just to get your name in the paper. Well, it worked."

A couple of insurance companies had called—two old clients who'd read the article. Maybe they admired my citizenship, or maybe they just realized I hadn't dropped off the edge of the earth.

Both companies had some routine work. Mostly taking around release forms for doctors to sign and picking up records. Doctors are notorious for being too busy to respond by mail. I made appointments, then called Rita back to bum a shower.

"Sure," she said. "You want to stay for lunch?"

Rita has lost twenty-five pounds, gained a boyfriend named Farley, and become a vegetarian. Lunch would be some concoction of seaweed and garbanzo beans, maybe Tofutti for dessert. I am constitutionally unable to eat ice cream made out of bean curd, so I said, "Gee, thanks, I can't today."

"Coward," she said.

With two paying customers on tap, I put the whole Morales mess on hold, locked the office door, and changed my clothes. Then I made a quick stop in the ladies' room to lipstick my mouth, brush on some blush and—what the heck, might as well shoot the works. I penciled on some eyeliner and stood back for a critical look.

Cheryl Tiegs wouldn't miss any sleep, but worry and restricted funds keep my weight to a trim 118. Rita keeps suggesting blond highlights for my brown hair. Farley says henna. I'll keep it the way it is, something like the color of a cinnamon stick. Matches my eyes. Jack used to say they looked like the bottom of a beer bottle, Budweiser not Heineken.

The memory was a sucker punch, unexpected and painful enough to make my throat close up. But I was making progress. At least I hadn't ruined my eye makeup.

The insurance companies took the rest of the day. I was back in my office by five. A check with Rita told me no more miracles had occurred. Oh, well. Maybe tomorrow I would call every insurance company in Los Angeles, spend my days sitting in doctors' offices. Not much money, but it would pay the bills.

I kicked off my shoes, made some coffee, wondered if I could afford more than a candy bar for dinner.

The phone rang. This time it was Arlene Simpson.

"I wondered—have you had time to think about helping my son, Miss West?"

"Not really," I hedged. "I've been so busy right now with clients and—"

"I'm sorry. I don't mean to bug you. It's just—they had the arraignment and Mike says it's useless. He says they need somebody to pin this on and he's it. He tries to act so tough, but he's not—not inside. If you could just see him, talk to him—"

I knew I should say no, absolutely not, hang up and leave it alone. If Morales's attorney was any good at all, he'd point out to a jury that I hadn't really *seen* anything. Maybe he'd make them believe it.

"Please, Miss West, I don't know what we're going to do if you don't help us."

"I can't see your son," I began firmly, then hesitated. "But I suppose I could talk to his attorney. What was his name again?"

The woman who answered the phone at the Public Defender's Office said that Mr. Scott was on his way out, but maybe she could catch him. There was a long pause, then a male voice said, "This is Matthew Scott."

"Mr. Scott, my name is Delilah West. I understand you're defending Michael Morales on the hit-and-run charge. I'd like to talk to you about it."

"I see. How about first thing tomorrow morning?"

"I'd rather come now, if it's possible."

"Frankly, Miss West, I don't intend to spend one more minute in this office for you or anybody else. However, I'm going directly to the Sundown Saloon. It's on Katella, a couple of blocks east of Disneyland. You're welcome to talk to me there. I'll be the tired-looking fella working on his second double Scotch."

It was well into the rush hour. I avoided the freeway and battled my way to Anaheim on the surface streets.

When I turned on Katella, Disneyland was just around the corner. I could see the artificial slopes of the Matterhorn looking strangely small against the high-rise hotels that had sprung up around it. I remembered coming here with my dad when the white pinnacle was the highest spot for miles around. Time and progress are hard on memories.

It was not exactly tourist weather, and most of the motels that lined Katella had vacancy signs. The Sundown Saloon was easy to find. The name was spelled out in neon against weathered wood, and it came complete with board sidewalks and hitching rails.

Inside, the place was one big room, dimly lit, with a massive bar along one wall and a cheerful, beery smell. A wavy mirror hung behind the bar along with a mounted deer-head, a seven-point buck with glassy eyes that looked as if it had been bagged just across the way in Frontierland. On the jukebox a female voice twanged its way through a lament that told of dirty dishes, unruly kids, and a husband sleeping in another woman's bed.

A couple of urban cowboys at the bar wore Calvin Klein jeans, Yves St. Laurent shirts, and four-hundred-dollar boots, but mostly the patrons were weary businessmen having one for the road.

Rough-sawn tables filled the rest of the room. There was only one man sitting alone, so I headed over. He stood up as I approached.

About forty, I thought. Five nine or ten. If I wore heels, we'd be almost eye to eye. The collar of his white shirt was unbuttoned, and his necktie dangled from the pocket of the conservative gray suit coat he had slung on the back of his chair.

"Mr. Scott?" I asked.

"You must be Delilah West," he said. "Please sit down, and make it Matt. I like to leave the formalities at the office."

He helped me off with my coat, and I had a moment to study him as we settled into the calico-covered cushions of the heavy wooden chairs. He had a bony, angular face, softened by mild gray eyes. A thatch of dark-brown hair curled around his ears and over his collar.

A waitress in a brief denim skirt, fringed shirt, and cowboy boots came over, and I told her, "Just coffee, black."

After she left, Matt lifted his glass and studied me over the rim. "You like country music?"

"Do you?"

"Yep," he admitted cheerfully. "After a day of whereases and therefores, I find it refreshingly straightforward."

"It's that, all right."

The waitress came back with a Thermos server and a cup and saucer. After she left, I said, "You do know my connection with the Morales case?"

"Of course. I recognized your name. What did you want to discuss with me?"

"His mother came to see me this afternoon."

He waited, saying nothing.

"She's got some crazy idea about hiring me to find out who killed Mr. Collins. According to her, it was definitely not her son."

"Was she serious?" When I nodded, he gave me a quirky smile. "A unique idea, a witness trying to prove she was wrong."

"The whole thing's ridiculous," I said, not sure if I was angry with him or myself.

"Is it?" he asked softly. "Then why are you here? Second thoughts?"

"I'm here because I'm a sucker for a sob story, that's all. Listen, do you have the results of the autopsy on Mr. Collins?"

"Not yet. Just the preliminary report."

"How about forensics?"

"No. What exactly are you looking for?"

"I don't know." I stared down at my coffee.

And then I remembered.

"Don't you have one little doubt?" Arlene Simpson had asked. I did. An infinitesimally small one. But a doubt.

FOUR

Of the three buildings that occupy the block on Flower between 5th and 6th, the men's jail is the biggest unit. It's bracketed by two smaller facilities: the women's jail and the headquarters for the Orange County Sheriff's Department.

The architect had done his best to camouflage the purpose of the complex. An abstract motif, kind of a Greek key design, circles the square concrete building. Since the slots in the pattern are windows, there's no need for bars. During the day, inmates can look out through the skinny holes and see a wide expanse of lawn, huge trees, even a small rose garden. But it was dark now, a cold darkness that made the building look exactly like what it was: a prison.

I parked behind Matt's old MG on 6th and we walked together, saying little as we went inside. My request to visit his client hadn't surprised him. I had a feeling nothing much did. He consented, but warned, "I'll stop the interview cold any time I think you're going too far."

While we waited in a small room, I wondered why all jails, regardless of size and cleanliness, feel and smell the same.

The door opened, and a uniformed guard brought in a lanky boy dressed in jeans and a sweatshirt. Blotchy skin, greasy hair, muddy brown eyes...I decided the news photo had flattered him.

He raked me with a contemptuous look and said to Matt, "What's she doing here? Hey, man, like I don't have to talk to no social worker."

"Ms. West's not a social worker. Listen, Mike, this whole thing is pretty unusual, and you're just going to have to trust my judgment, okay? Remember the witness who reported the hit and run?"

"Yeah. Some woman named—" He broke off and stared at me, then turned on Matt. "What the fuck's the matter with you, man? You're supposed to be my lawyer, protect my rights, shit like that. It's not enough she turned me in, she's gotta come down here and gloat?"

"Mike, why don't you sit down and listen," Matt said quietly. "If I thought this could harm your case, I wouldn't have brought her here."

Mike didn't like it, but he sat, glaring at both of us.

"This isn't easy for me either," I said. "And I wouldn't be here, but your mother came to see me today."

He blinked with surprise. "Mom? What for?"

"To hire me to prove you didn't kill Mr. Collins."

"That's crazy." He studied me, figuring the angles. "Why would you want to prove yourself a liar?"

"Not a liar. Mistaken, maybe. Did I make a mistake?"

"You sure as hell did. Not that it matters," he said bitterly. "There's no way I'm getting out of this. I can't even raise bail. The judge made sure of that. And my lawyer here, he's talking about plea bargaining."

"It's part of my job to tell you about your options," Matt said. "Now calm down, and tell Ms. West what happened."

The boy hunched his bony shoulders and stared at his skinned knuckles and black-rimmed nails. "I worked at the garage until eleven. I was on my way home. The street was wet, and I skidded out. I shoulda stopped, but I saw you get up, and I figured you were all right. And like, I was scared. So, I just kept going. I never saw the old man."

"Mr. Collins didn't wander out into the street in front of you?"

"No," he said vehemently.

"But you did run over him."

"No." This time the word carried no conviction.

"I was there, remember?"

"Hold it," Matt said. "He told you his story, Delilah. Don't say anything else, Mike."

"He doesn't have to," I said. "I know what happened. You see, Mike, I figured Mr. Collins walked out into the street and you hit him, but something kept bothering me."

I explained what I finally realized was that the sequence of sounds was wrong. If somebody steps in front of your car, you go for the brakes. What I heard was first the sound of the car rolling over the body and *then* the brakes. "I think Mr. Collins was already lying there in the road, but you did run over him, didn't you?"

"I don't know. Honest to God, I don't. I was tuning the radio. I never saw anything. There was this bump and it startled me so I really slammed it on, and then I lost it and almost hit you, but—"

"Michael," Matt said sharply.

"—but I thought I ran over a tree limb or something," he went on, unheeding. "But now—now I keep thinking, what if he *was* there, like he fell down or fainted or like maybe he had a stroke, and what if I really did…Holy Mother of God, how am I ever gonna know for sure?"

Bang, the shutters came down. He jumped up, jammed his hands in his pockets, and said, "Fuck this." He went over and hammered on the door.

"Mike, wait a minute," Matt said.

"Fuck off, man. So we all feel sorry for poor old Mike. What's the difference? I'm gonna take the fall, so just leave me alone, okay?"

The guard came in, looked at Matt.

Matt nodded. "It's all right. We've finished." When the door closed behind them, he said, "That boy doesn't make it easy, does he? Now, as for you, Ms. West." There was a chill in his eyes to match his formal tone. "You know damn well I'll never let you repeat what he said to you in court."

"I didn't think you would. That doesn't change things. He did run over Mr. Collins."

"But he didn't necessarily kill him. That's why you asked about the autopsy, wasn't it?"

I nodded.

"Come on," he said. "Let's find a telephone, and I'll check in with the coroner's office."

I waited in the reception area while he made the call. When he came back, his face was grim. "It's still preliminary, but Joseph Collins's chest was crushed. Also, he had massive cerebral hemorrhaging. The coroner can't pin down which injury was the cause of death."

"Cerebral hemorrhage…a blow to the head?"

"Or hitting the pavement after he was struck by a car."

So the autopsy wasn't going to give me a way out. I was never going to know what happened to Joseph Collins unless I found out for myself.

It started to rain as Matt and I left the county jail. We hurried down to the street, buttoning up raincoats and peering into the watery darkness. I was hungry and cold and faced with the prospect of sitting alone in my office.

"How about some dinner?" I said. "If you don't have plans."

"I'd like to, but I've got to be in court early. Stay in touch, okay?" Head down, he made a run for his car.

I watched him drive off, rain trickling down my collar. My social life was as big a mess as my career. Time to do something about it, but meanwhile, I still had to eat. Freeway traffic had thinned considerably and, in spite of the rain, I made it to Al's Place in ten minutes.

Red neon promised breakfast twenty-four hours a day, and there was plenty of parking for big semis. I found a spot between Global

Van Lines and Mobil Oil and splashed my way toward the entrance. Al's Place was a nondescript beige rectangle with beer signs decorating steamy plate-glass windows. The inside was strictly functional: tile floors, Formica tables, vinyl-covered chairs. There was a smell of frying onions and wet clothes. Dishes clattered and waitresses yelled their orders. Made me feel right at home.

I didn't see Arlene Simpson, but, as I slipped out of my raincoat and headed for the counter, she backed through the swinging door to the kitchen, plates of food stacked up to her elbows.

She stopped briefly, the look of surprise on her face giving way to a combination of hope and dread. "Miss West? Listen, I'll be right back. I just gotta serve this and—"

"No rush," I told her.

She dealt out the food to three men at a corner table and hurried over. "I didn't expect to see you so soon. I mean, you said you'd think about it and—did you? Think about it?"

"I went to see your son," I said.

She tensed. "You did? I wish you'd told me you were going. He's not very good with strangers, and sometimes when he's so upset he has such a smart mouth. I'm not saying that excuses him, understand. But if you could just take it into account, Miss West—"

"I do," I assured her.

"You do? You mean you're going to help us? You'll take the case?"

Much as I hated to dim the glow of happiness on her face, I had to set things straight. "I don't really consider this a case, Mrs. Simpson. But I do have some doubts. Enough to make me want to do some checking around."

"Well, sure. Whatever you want. But I know you'll find out that Mike didn't kill that old man. Oh, this is just wonderful, Mrs. West, but listen—I'm standing here rattling on, and I'll bet you'd like some coffee, wouldn't you?"

While she plied me with coffee and Al's double bacon cheese-burger with a side of onion rings, I tried to get through to her that I still wasn't promising anything.

She kept nodding and saying she understood, but that shining look in her eyes told me she had prayed for a miracle, and as far as she was concerned, I was the one who was going to deliver it.

I spent a restless night in my sleeping bag wondering what the hell I'd gotten myself into. I had zero experience as a miracle worker. Clear Michael Morales of the hit-and-run charge? Oh, sure. Only maybe I'd better practice up first. Something easy. Like walking on water.

I didn't even know where to begin, so I decided to keep it simple and answer a question that bothered me right from the start. Why was Mr. Collins out walking that night? There was something else that bothered me too, but sleep drifted in, fuzzing up my thoughts. I didn't want to think about it anyway because I knew what I had to do.

I had to go and talk with Joseph Collins's family.

FIVE

Next morning, I got up early and went over to Jorge Sanchez's house for a shower and *huevos rancheros* with Consuelo and the kids before she took the children to school and went to work. Jorge was long gone. Most days he gets to Mom's at five-thirty. I know a few words of Spanish, and Consuelo knows a few words of English. The kids chatter away in both languages so we get along just fine.

I saw them off, insisting on staying to clean up the kitchen, and had a few minutes for a last cup of coffee alone in a real house. I didn't even mind washing dishes.

Back at the office, I straightened up and hid the sleeping bag. Got out the list of doctors I had to see and made up a mental chart of the most practical route. I was about ready to leave when Charlie called.

He'd read about the hit and run in the paper. "You okay?" he asked.

Aside from scabby knees, I told him I was just fine.

"Well, I guess this'll be pretty much an open-and-shut case against the driver," he said. "Lucky you could give them a description."

"Yeah," I said. "Lucky."

"The foot's okay? The one you hurt at the mall?"

I assured him it was fine. He seemed to be having trouble ending the conversation so I finally said I had to get going. He rang off—reluctantly, I thought. And wondered why he was so concerned. Maybe he owed Jack more than I'd ever realized.

Dressed for success in a nonthreatening beige suit and a cocoa blouse, I took my list of physicians and went out to the parking lot just as Lieutenant Brady drove in.

He pulled up, blocking my car, and rolled down his window. "Miss West, I heard about your trip down to the jail last night."

"It wasn't a secret. What about it?"

"Damned peculiar thing to do. First you finger this kid for us and then you're having a confab with him and his P.D. What's that all about?"

"His mother thinks he's innocent. She asked me to talk to him."

"Uh-huh. And what do you think? You changing your story?"

"No." Not yet anyway. "Look, Lieutenant, I'd like to stand and chat but I'm running late—"

He gave me a surly grunt and drove off. Well, what did I expect? Hard enough to get a clean bust. Of course he was annoyed at the idea I might mess it up.

By two o'clock I decided I'd exposed myself to enough coughs and sneezes and God knows what for one day. Or maybe I was just depressed. A couple of the doctors were obstetricians. Thirty-five's not old but the sight of all those round, awkward women tuned me in to the biological clock ticking away inside me.

If Jack had lived...well, he hadn't. And, face it, chances are he'd never have talked me into having a baby. I just don't see myself as the motherly type.

After a fish sandwich at McDonald's—I eat at only the best places these days—I went back to my office and checked in with Rita. Arlene Simpson had called. So had an attorney with a job offer. Serving subpoenas—no, thanks.

As for Arlene...

Reluctantly I took out the phone book.

As I drove up winding streets toward the Jacobs residence in Anaheim Hills, the clouds moved off and the sun came out. Everything had a bright clean look. The gray-green eucalyptus sparkled, the damp leaves smelling like Noxzema.

According to the obituary column, Joseph Collins's funeral had been held this morning, a private ceremony, contributions in lieu of flowers to be sent to the American Cancer Society. If I was lucky, the family would be at home now, all together. Lucky—that word again.

I'd changed to my navy skirt and a matching blazer, white-ascot-tied blouse and navy shoes, properly sober and sympathetic.

At the cross street, two feet of brickwork buttressed both sides of the road and announced in ornate lettering: Cresta Verde. It sounded California Spanish, but maybe the builder was schizo, because the large houses on estate-size lots looked French: mansard roofs with dormers, small-paned windows, a lot of blue trim.

Parked in the Jacobs's circular driveway was a Mercedes, a Nissan Z, and a Jaguar. Carrying out the international theme, an old Chevy sat on a graveled space, partially hidden, beside the garage. I added my Mustang and walked up to the carved front door.

A young woman answered the bell, saying "I'll get it, Nguyet" over her shoulder.

I caught a glimpse of an Asian woman coming into the entry, then quickly retreating. The girl who opened the door said, "Yes? Can I help you?"

I guessed she was in her late teens, some ten pounds too heavy for these anorexic times. Her light-brown hair was pulled into a knot on top of her head, and she wore an unflattering black cotton dress. Her best feature was her eyes. They were huge, that shade of china blue that's not quite a pastel. But the whites were red-streaked, the lids swollen.

"I'd like to speak to Mrs. Pamela Jacobs," I said. "Is she home?"

"Yes, but I'm sorry, she's—I mean, there's been a—a death in the family."

"I know. I'm Delilah West. I found your grandfather the night of the—" I hesitated over the word, finally chose "—accident. I wanted to pay my respects."

Her blue eyes filled with fresh tears. "Oh, please, come in. I know my mother will—"

"Carolyn?"

We both turned. A woman stood in the wide doorway, slender and elegant in charcoal silk, her long black hair twisted and secured by a thin silver clasp.

"Oh, Carolyn, for God's sake." She advanced into the entry hall with quick staccato steps. Compared to her mother's, Carolyn's soft, childish body seemed graceless and lumpy, and I was sure Carolyn knew it.

"I'm sorry." Pamela had a soft, full mouth but her eyes were a cold gray. "I can't see anyone right now."

"But, Mother," Carolyn said. "This is Miss West. You know— the lady the newspaper said...the lady who found Grandpa."

"I see." Pamela looked me over. Evidently I passed inspection, because I got a regal nod. "I'm sorry, Miss West. We've had so many press people, complete strangers poking around. Come in for a minute, please."

She led the way to a large, airy living room. Antique furniture looked newly upholstered, the blues and greens echoed in the soft colors of an Aubusson rug spread in front of a massive fireplace. French doors stood open, revealing a flagstone patio, bright with sunshine and pots of yellow daisies.

A man walked in from the patio, but I got only a glimpse of him because Carolyn stopped dead in front of me, and I had to do some maneuvering to keep from running into her.

"Why's he still here?" Carolyn demanded. "Where's Daddy?"

I eased around her, curious to see who she hated so much. A tall man in a dark, three-piece suit, light-blue shirt, and dark tie with a modest red stripe.

"Carolyn." The way Pamela said it made her daughter flush.

"Maybe I'd better go," the man said.

Mid-forties, I thought. He moved like an athlete. Something kept him in shape. I guessed tennis. His tanned, pleasant face was topped by thinning beige hair, carefully styled to hide a receding hairline.

"No, Warren. Don't be silly. Carolyn, your father went to South Coast to open the store. You'd think today of all days he could close the place but—" Pamela broke off, forced a tight smile. "Sorry, Miss West, but we're all on edge. Especially Carolyn. She was very close to her grandfather."

She paused, shot a look at Carolyn, who muttered, "Sorry," then Pamela offered coffee and introduced the man as Warren Kurtz who managed Collins Electronics.

"Warren," she said, "Miss West is the one who found Dad."

"Oh, yes. Of course. Miss West, I'm glad you came by. Why don't we all sit down."

Warren touched my elbow, deftly steering me to a pair of loveseats arranged to face each other in front of a fireplace. He sat beside me, leaving the opposite sofa for Pamela and Carolyn. Good move. Seeing him sitting next to her mother would only antagonize Carolyn more.

Currents and cross-currents zapped around like laser beams as Carolyn brought me a cup and a saucer, bone china, a delicate white against the deep brown of the steaming coffee.

"Thank you for trying to help Joe, Miss West." Warren's voice dropped a couple of registers, became deep and vibrant.

"I'm afraid there wasn't much I could do," I said.

"At least you tried," Carolyn said.

"Yes, we're very grateful," Pamela said. "And thank God you helped the police catch that horrible little creep who ran him down. If he was still out there, free—"

"Well, he's not," Warren said soothingly. "Did you hear, Miss West? The Morales boy couldn't raise bail."

"I know." I drank some coffee, trying to think of some brilliant way to ask why Mr. Collins was out on the street that night.

Then Pamela said, "One thing still bothers me. I can't imagine what Dad was doing out so late."

"A walk, probably," Warren said. "You know how Joe liked his walks."

"I suppose you're right, but—"

"If you'd gone to see him more often, maybe you'd know," Carolyn burst out. "He might have been getting sick, or—or—"

"Carolyn, that's ridiculous. Your grandfather was here for dinner two nights before he died and he was fine."

"Then you must be blind. I saw him last Monday, and I'm sure he was upset about something. Of course you don't pay any attention to anybody anymore except—" She stood up, tears running down her face, and bolted the room.

"Oh, God. That girl," Pamela said.

"Maybe you should go after her," Warren said.

"It wouldn't do any good. Miss West, I apologize. My father's death was so sudden—"

She broke off and reached for a decanter that sat on a silver tray at the end of the coffee table. She filled a wineglass with the tawny liquid—sherry, I guessed—and took a long swallow. Her tanned skin looked chalky.

Pamela Jacobs was hurting, I decided. She just kept it all inside, tightly controlled. Suddenly I felt like the sleaziest member of my profession. There was a name they called us years ago. Peeper. Somebody who peered into dirty back windows looking for dirty little secrets.

I stood up. "This is a bad time for you, so I won't intrude any longer. I just want to say you have my sympathy."

Pamela murmured something, tired, relieved that I was going.

"I'll show you out," Warren said.

He walked beside me to the door, a large, comforting presence. Is that what he was to Pamela? Was Carolyn reading something into the relationship that wasn't there? I hadn't seen much, a look or two, nothing to base a judgment on, but somehow I went along with Carolyn's instincts.

"Thanks for coming, Miss West. I know Pam appreciates it." He opened the door and then I was out in the sunshine.

Driving away, past the turn into the Cresta Verde entrance, I saw Carolyn. There were no sidewalks, and she was walking, head down, in the narrow, winding road. I slowed to a crawl and called her name.

She kept plodding along, so I stopped, set the hand brake, and got out.

"Carolyn?"

She turned to stare at me, her eyes blank, unfocused. It was cold in the shade, and a sudden gust of wind rattled the trees. She had left the house without a sweater or a jacket. Her skin felt cold as I touched her arm. I took off my coat and put it around her shoulders.

"Carolyn," I said gently. "Come get in the car, and I'll take you back to the house."

I led her to the Mustang, keeping an eye open for approaching vehicles. A good place to get rear-ended, and I didn't relax until I got the car moving again.

"That was a dumb thing to do." I kept one eye on the rearview mirror as I found a place to turn around.

"I guess so," she said dully. Long straight strands of hair had worked free of the knot and hung around her face. "I was going to take the car, but I forgot my purse and I didn't have the keys."

"Thank God for that much. Carolyn, what you said earlier about your grandfather being upset—do you know what was bothering him?"

"*He* was here." No need to ask who she meant.

"That's all it was—just Warren being here for dinner?"

"No—I don't know. I think maybe it was that place he lived. It's so creepy. I kept telling him he ought to move here with us. If he had, if I'd talked him into it—"

"Oh, Carolyn, it's real easy to lay that kind of guilt trip on your-self. Believe me, I know." I pulled into the Jacobses' driveway. "Look, you're hurting now, but it will get better.

"I don't think so," she said bleakly. "My mother—she'll have Grandpa's money now, and I know what she'll do. She'll get a divorce. So you see, Miss West, it won't get better at all."

SIX

I drove down the hilly streets, deciding what to do next. I had a couple of choices. Seeing Kenneth Jacobs was one. His wife had said he was at his store at South Coast. I didn't know what kind of business she meant, but it sounded as though it was located in South Coast Plaza. If so, I could easily find out. I'd gotten to know the head of security during my stint at May Company.

But the other possibility was nearer, and it might be a better bet.

Linda Vista Park formed a buffer zone between the small businesses along Arbor and a residential section where single-family tracts were slowly being infiltrated by apartment buildings and condominiums. In the late-afternoon sunshine, the grass was a lush spring green.

I parked along the sidewalk in front of the retirement hotel where Mr. Collins had lived.

Terrace Towers was an older three-story building with a graceful arch of jacaranda trees hiding a plain buff-colored exterior. The lobby was spacious with a faint air of shabbiness and a smell of stale air. The floor was gray tile that managed to look dull even though it was shiny. A large fig tree drooped in a small woven straw cachepot. Silk, I saw, and it needed dusting. What had Carolyn said? Creepy. I thought of a few other descriptive words: stodgy, staid, and—well, yes, creepy.

The reception desk was deserted, but just behind it was a door marked Manager, partially ajar. I could hear voices coming from the room, so I waited and looked around.

A large bulletin board hung next to the elevators, its cork surface covered with notices that offered participation in every hobby from poker to tatting lace. Just reading the lists made me tired: gourmet cooking, backgammon, square dancing. And for the social-minded, something called Greenspace. A blurb read: *Work for a clean environment.*

The manager's door opened, and a man's voice said, "And get Interstate Food Supply for me, Doris. Damn mess, that's what it is," to the woman who came out with a stack of file folders in her arms.

Mid-fifties, I guessed, with a full figure tamed by boned bras and girdles. When she saw me, she smiled a bright, professional smile—the kind that can hide anything from an ingrown toenail to an alcoholic husband.

"Hello," she said. "Can I help you?"

A plastic name plate told me it was Doris Beardsley who sat behind this desk eight hours a day, saying "Good morning," listening to complaints and plans, watching people come and go.

"I hope so."

I handed her a card. Not mine, of course. One I'd picked up yesterday just in case she'd read the papers and would remember my name.

"Miss—Ames?"

"Of California Life," I said. "I'm investigating the death of Joseph Collins."

"Mr. Collins? I don't understand. I thought the police arrested that Mexican boy."

"It's strictly routine. Mr. Collins carried a large policy with us, and I have to fill out a report." Everybody understands reports.

"Well, I don't know if Mr. Hernandez can talk to you right now. There was some mix-up in the food deliveries. If you'd like to make an appointment for later…"

"To tell you the truth, Mrs. Beardsley," I said with a candid smile, "I'd rather talk to you. I'm sure you're the one who really knows the people who live here. So if I could just ask you a few questions?"

Flattered, she nodded her consent and I sat down.

I said that what I'd like was a picture of Mr. Collins's movements the night he was killed. She told me she coordinated the social activities and was always around until nine-thirty, but she hadn't seen Mr. Collins that night after dinner.

"He didn't participate in any of the activities?"

"Very few. He played poker once in a while. Oh, and I think he was a member of Greenspace, but that's not one of our projects. They meet over at the clubhouse in the park."

"Was there a meeting that night?"

"I don't know. There could've been."

A meeting might account for his being near the park. But where were the rest of the club members? I certainly hadn't seen anybody else around, and no signs of activity.

"Don't you have anybody on duty here? Some kind of system to keep track of people coming and going?"

"Miss Ames, this isn't a nursing home. Our residents may have a few problems, but for the most part they can take care of themselves and we don't keep tabs on them."

"So there's no security guard or doorman?"

"No. These doors are locked at eight o'clock. After that the residents let themselves in. As far as security, Mr. Hernandez lives in the building, so he's available if he's needed. We also have a resident nurse and a doctor on call."

She sounded more and more defensive, so I said soothingly, "I'm sure you're handling things just fine, Mrs. Beardsley. I just want to find out if anybody saw Mr. Collins leave that night. What about his friends? You said he played poker once in a while."

She nodded. "I can give you their names. There's also Mrs. Taylor. Lucy Taylor. They both belonged to Greenspace, and I think he saw quite a bit of her."

She thumbed a Rolodex and wrote names and room numbers on a note pad. "I don't know how much luck you'll have finding people in just now. There was a trip downtown today to see a matinee.

A musical." She looked up with an amused smile. "*The Best Little Whorehouse in Texas.*"

As she tore off the sheet of paper and handed it to me, the intercom buzzed. She tilted her head toward the elevator and said, "House phone's over there," as she picked up the receiver. I mouthed a thank-you and left her to reassure her boss that no, she hadn't forgotten to call Interstate Food Supply and yes, of course, she understood how serious it was.

I worked my way through the poker players with no success. Mrs. Lucy Taylor was last on the list. Her phone rang only twice before she picked it up. She was reluctant, but when I told her she could check me out with Doris Beardsley, she agreed to talk to me.

Her apartment was on the second floor, in the back near the fire stairs. I knocked on the door, and while I waited for her to answer, I noticed how quiet it was in the building. I hoped it was because they were a horny old bunch and eager to see the action down at the Chicken Ranch. I hated to think there was always this funereal pall of silence.

I heard the tap-tap of footsteps on the other side of the door and fixed a smile on my face to rival Mrs. Beardsley's.

The door opened. "Miss Ames?"

I blinked and stared, my mouth hanging open.

The last time I'd seen the little old lady standing in front of me, she had been running through the Christmas shoppers at South Coast Plaza while I crashed into a planter.

"You are Miss Ames?" No answering flash of recognition in her soft blue eyes.

"Uh, yes. Right." Could I be mistaken? Same silver hair curled around a pink-cheeked face. Something was slightly different, but I couldn't think what it was. "Thanks for seeing me, Mrs. Taylor."

"Please come in, dear, and call me Lucy. I'm seventy-three years old, but when anybody calls me Mrs. Taylor, I still look around for my mother-in-law. What's your first name, dear?"

"Delilah," I said, the word out before I could catch it. Sharon Ames was on the business card. Had I given her a first name on the phone?

If I had, she didn't notice. She just said, "Delilah—so pretty and old-fashioned," and took a step back from the door, giving me another surprise. She carried a cane and leaned on it heavily as she limped across the living room to a sofa. Certainly not the spry old woman I'd chased through the mall, unless…

"I see you've sprained your ankle." I took an easy chair next to the sofa.

"I'm afraid it's more than that, but I shouldn't complain. Compared to what happened to poor Joe…His funeral was this morning. I wanted to go, but it was private, just for the family. It doesn't seem right somehow, not to—not to say good-bye to him." She fumbled in the pocket of her lavender print dress for a lace-edged hanky.

I tried to imagine her heisting it from Scarves and Accessories, but the image just didn't play. I'd never actually been face to face with the woman. Could I make a positive I.D. in court? Maybe not.

To make up for my nasty suspicions, I said gently, "I'm sure he would understand. You were good friends?"

She nodded and wiped her eyes. "We had tea right here in this room the day he died."

"What time was he here, Mrs. Taylor?"

"Lucy, dear. Please."

"Lucy."

"Why, let me see. It was after lunch. Around two o'clock."

I looked around the apartment. The couch served as a divider between living and eating areas. The place was decorated in browns and oranges that were a shade too bright, deliberately cheerful. A painting in the same color scheme, motel-room art, hung over a tiny table scaled to go with the kitchenette. I pictured the two of them sitting there, chatting.

"How did Mr. Collins seem to you?" I asked. "Was he feeling all right?"

"Oh, yes. Joe was hardly ever sick."

"How long had you known him?"

"Only about six months—that's when I moved here. But somehow it seems longer."

"His granddaughter thought he was upset about something. That maybe he wasn't happy living here. Did he ever mention anything to you?"

"Heavens, no. I don't know why she'd think that. Joe loved it here. He had so many friends. He was such an active man, so full of life. It's these kids today, Delilah—these awful kids running wild and taking dope and—and—"

I could see another flood of tears coming. "Lucy, can I get you something?" I spotted a kettle on the stove. "How about some tea?"

"That would be nice. But I should be making it for you."

"No, please. Sit there. I'll be happy to do it."

After I put the kettle on, she kept up a patter of instructions for locating a tray, cups and saucers, loose tea leaves that went into a little stainless infusor…"I do like it so much better than tea bags, don't you, dear?"…spoons, a sugar bowl.

When I brought it all over and set it on the coffee table, she smiled. "My, isn't this nice? Joe and I used to do this almost every day."

"That last time you had tea together—did he tell you his plans for the rest of the day?"

"Why, yes, some of them. He was going over to Collins Electronics—that's the company he used to own, you know. He had an appointment to see Mr. Kurtz, the manager."

Interesting, I thought. Warren Kurtz hadn't mentioned that he'd seen Mr. Collins that day, but why should he? And my brilliant questioning certainly hadn't uncovered the information.

"Did Joe say why he was going to see Mr. Kurtz?" I asked.

"No, I don't think so, but then I didn't ask. Would you mind pouring the tea, dear? I'm afraid I've misplaced my glasses and... what was I saying?"

"His appointment with Kurtz," I prompted, filling the cups and offering the sugar bowl.

"Oh, I remember. He said it was something important, but he didn't say what. I thought it might be personal."

I could think of one thing that might be personal between him and Warren. "His daughter?"

She looked startled. "You've met Pam? Well, of course, she must be the beneficiary—" It wasn't quite a question. I gave her a non-committal smile, and she went on, "Then you must have met Ken too."

"No. He was at work."

"I've met Ken several times when he was visiting Joe. Such a nice man. Joe was very fond of him. He and Pam—well, there were problems. I know Joe was worried about it. I thought he might want to talk, but it's always so busy during dinner, and then later he went to the Greenspace meeting."

"There was a meeting? In the park clubhouse?"

"Yes, at eight o'clock. I wanted to go, but my leg was bothering me, and it was raining. So I stayed home."

"Do you know what time the meeting ended?"

"Around ten, I think. At least that was the usual time. Maybe if I'd gone..." Her mouth trembled again. "—Maybe he would've come back here with me instead of going for a walk and—"

So that's how it happened. It was as simple as that. A meeting in the park and then he went for a walk to clear his head and...

"It was raining," I said.

The sidewalks along Linda Vista Park had been littered with leaves and coated with mud, but Joseph Collins's polished shoe had been shiny in the strobe of emergency flashers. Shiny and clean. Very clean.

Whatever Joseph Collins had been doing just before he died, he had not been walking along that muddy sidewalk in Linda Vista Park.

SEVEN

"Dear, are you all right?" Lucy peered at me over her cup.

"Fine."

If Mr. Collins hadn't walked down Arbor that meant somebody else had put him there in the street…

Murder?

If so, then Mike was telling the truth.

"Lucy, did Joe have any enemies?"

"Enemies?" She stared at me, and for a moment her misty blue eyes were oddly opaque. "My goodness, what a strange question. Everybody liked Joe. Surely there's no doubt that Morales boy killed him. There was a witness."

"I know," I said, then added quickly, "just routine questions."

I apologized for taking up her time and asked for a name and telephone number for Greenspace.

"Yes, of course. Amy Ferguson runs the organization. I've got my address book right here…" She found it on the end table, flipped a few pages and said, "I really do need my glasses. Do you see them around here, dear? I can't imagine where I put them."

I took a look and found them on the floor in the small space between the couch and the end table. Round, wire-rimmed, the kind appropriately called granny glasses.

As she put them on, her smile of thanks froze in place and her skin turned pasty. Her instant recognition—and the fact that the glasses filled in my memory of her—told me I'd been right in the first place. She *was* my fleet-footed old shoplifter, the one who got away.

"You—you're the one who—that day in the mall—" She fumbled for her cane, tried to stand up, swayed precariously.

I eased her back on the sofa, ignoring her whimpers of protest, alarmed by her pallor and rapid breathing. She needed something stronger than tea.

"Lucy, sit there. Relax. It's all right."

I went into the kitchenette, opened cupboards until I found some liquor. "Here." I poured brandy. "Drink some of this."

"Don't call the police—please—everybody will know and—"

"Drink," I commanded, "and listen to me. As far as I'm concerned the incident in the mall is over. In order to bring charges, I would have had to catch you outside the store with the merchandise in your possession. And we both know I blew it."

The reassurances helped. So did the brandy. Her cheeks got pink and her breathing improved.

"I was so scared," she said. "Scared to death. Please, dear, I want to tell you about it. To explain."

"It's not necessary."

"But you have to understand." She held the glass with both hands, took a long swallow. "My husband was a wonderful, generous man." They were comfortable, middle class, and when her husband died there was insurance. But there was also inflation and medical bills that Medicare didn't cover. "I have my annuity and some Social Security so I can live here and eat, but that's about all. I know it's a lot more than most people have and I do try to accept it, but sometimes—"

"You steal."

She flinched and nodded. "Just little things. Gifts, mostly. It's so hard, especially at Christmas with everybody giving things and…well, it's wrong. It's terribly wrong and I don't do it anymore. Actually, you know, I can thank you for that."

"Me?"

"Yes. That day—when you almost caught me—well, I got down on my knees and promised God I'd never do anything like that again. And I won't, dear, you must believe me."

"I'll hold you to it. Are you all right now? Do you need a doctor?"

"No, I'm fine." She gave me a tremulous smile. "Well, I'm not—not really. But I will be. I'd just like to rest now."

"That's a good idea. If I could have that phone number for Greenspace—"

"Of course." She found the number in her address book. "You won't change your mind—about the police, I mean."

"I gave you my word," I said, but she didn't look convinced at all.

Which might not be such a bad thing. If she stayed scared, maybe she'd think twice before shoplifting again.

After I left Terrace Towers, I went over to the park and found the clubhouse. A distracted young woman took a minute off from refereeing a fingerpainting class to tell me that Greenspace was not officially connected with the park. Other than the fact they used the clubhouse for meetings twice a month, she knew nothing about them. There was a telephone number—somewhere. She'd try to find it if I wanted to wait. I sidestepped a young artist with drippy green fingers, told her I had the number but thanks anyway, and beat a hasty retreat.

I double-checked the sidewalks. The one leading from the club-house to the street was slightly elevated with good drainage, nice and clean. By contrast, the grounds sloped down to the sidewalk that ran along the street. Ivy grew on the embankment, but when enough rain soaked into the earth, mud oozed out along the bottom. The sidewalk across the street was just as muddy.

I thought about other ways Mr. Collins could have gotten to the spot where he died without getting mud on his shoes. A car could have picked him up, then dropped him on Arbor where he was hit. But why? An argument? Did the old man get a sudden urge for some fresh air? It was possible—anything is possible. But I kept coming back to my first conclusion: Somebody killed him and dumped the body.

The sun had set, and it was cold and damp as I hurried back to my car. Of course there might be something I was missing here, something that could be filled in by the person who was the last one to see Mr. Collins before he died. Was it too late to call Greenspace?

A few fat raindrops splashed on the windshield as I looked for a phone booth. The Greenspace number rang for a good two minutes before I gave up. I thought about calling Matt Scott, but he was probably gone too and anyway, I might as well wait until I knew something for sure. Unless, of course, he'd called me. I dialed my office number to check in with Rita.

"West Detective Agency," a male voice said.

Either Rita had put Farley to work or—

"*Harry?* Harry, what the hell are you doing in my office?"

"Miz West? Why, I'm just up here fixing your air conditioner," he said virtuously.

"My *what*? In case you haven't noticed, it's forty-five degrees."

"I know that," he said in an injured tone. "Now's the time to fix things, Miz West, when you ain't using 'em. Anyway, I figured I'd do it while you were out of the office so I wouldn't be bothering you. Good thing I was here too. You had a whole bunch of phone calls. I wrote 'em all down for you and—"

"You've been answering my telephone? Harry, listen carefully." I closed my eyes and pressed my fingertips against my right temple, which was beginning to throb. "I have an answering service. That means they answer my phone, not you. So tell me who called and then you are never—repeat, NEVER—to answer my telephone again."

"Well, okay. You don't hafta shout. I got it all written down. Let's see…some guy from the electric company—Dancy? Yancy? Anyway, he said he wanted to give you an energy checkup. I told him your energy was just fine, thank you, and any checking up he wanted to do around here he'd just better see me first. Oh, then there was this really nice lady, had this book, *Karate in Ten Easy Lessons*. Sounded just the ticket for you..."

God, I don't believe this, I thought.

I was cold. I needed some aspirin. And a drink. A large drink. Instead I was standing in a leaky telephone booth listening to a crazy old man babble nonsense.

It was like taking in a scruffy little mongrel pup and tolerating the way he nips your fingers. Then one day he suddenly becomes an overgrown hound who bites you in the ankle.

Harry was still rattling away. The only name of any importance was Charlie Colfax. I finally shut Harry up and gave Charlie a call.

"Glad I caught you," Charlie said. "I've got another job for you, Delilah. Are you free for dinner?"

Charlie picked me up at seven in his Mercedes 450SL and we drove south, then west, getting off the freeway in Irvine and heading toward the coast. This part of the county used to smell like orange blossoms. Now the scent is money. High-rise banks at Fashion Island, big commercial complexes, housing developments with eye-popping price price tags.

A big percentage of all that wealth was owned by Erik Lundstrom, the client Charlie was taking me to meet. Charlie had dropped that little bomb as soon as I'd gotten into his car and then avoided a description of the job, saying "Oh, why don't we let Erik fill you in."

My wardrobe isn't exactly vast these days. I'd dithered between the beige suit and a plain black silk dress. Now I was glad I'd chosen the dress, but the silver chain with the silver-vermeil starfish ($3.95 on sale at Petrie's) was probably a mistake. I flipped down the visor again to check my hair in the mirror.

"You look fine," Charlie said.

"You don't think this is just a little bit weird? The guy's got so few friends he asks *us* for dinner?"

"What's wrong with us?"

"We play in the wrong league, Charlie."

Charlie gave me an amused glance.

"Well, I do, anyway," I said.

Just north of Laguna Beach, Charlie slowed and turned onto a narrow asphalt road. The headlights swept over sandstone boulders, tall grass, scrub oak, and holly as we twisted up through the low coastal hills.

"I heard a peculiar rumor today about your going to see the Morales kid," Charlie said. "What's the scoop?"

"A favor to his mother. She thinks he's innocent. Mothers always do."

I wasn't ready to admit that I'd gone out and dug into the case. I certainly wasn't ready to talk about the suspicion I had that somebody had killed Joseph Collins and left him there in the road, so I changed the subject. Probably a dumb conclusion, anyway. So what if his shoe was clean? Maybe the rain washed the mud off. But I couldn't help remembering my Reeboks. They'd been rained on too, but there was still mud in the grooves of the soles.

Along the road, pine and juniper replaced the native shrubs and there was some kind of dense, thorny undergrowth. I glimpsed a high stone wall behind this camouflage and then there was a gate ahead. It looked like something to keep cows from straying. A small shack housed the guard. Low key, but the guard himself was big and tough and well armed.

Charlie's electric window purred down, letting in cold damp air that smelled of the ocean and chaparral and rain. "Hi, Dave. He's expecting us."

"Evening, Mr. Colfax."

We got a little salute and the gate swung open. Another mile of augmented brush and then the road arced through broad lawns, circling in front of an enormous Spanish-style mansion, big enough to house Father Junipero Serra's entire mission at San Juan Capistrano.

We parked on the big brick-paved drive. There were a half-dozen other cars, including a Rolls, a Lamborghini, and a beat-up Jeep Cherokee. Rain pelted down, shining on the bricks. A man came out of the house with a big black umbrella and ran over to protect me as I got out.

"Watch your step," he said. "It's kind of slippery."

The butler? Valet?

"Hi, Erik," Charlie said, running around to shelter under the umbrella.

We made a snug little trio, splashing through the puddles toward the entrance. Inside, a smiling houseman collected our coats and the bumbershoot. He was about sixty, casually dressed, but there was no mistaking that he was a servant.

"Thanks, Ben," Erik Lundstrom said, then turned to us. "Come on in and sit by the fire."

Our host was tall, slender, hard muscled, dressed in old chinos and an L.L. Bean sweater, forest green, over a plaid shirt.

He led the way through the solid house. I glimpsed huge rooms, one that dwarfed a grand piano sitting at one end. Lots of artwork, mostly modern, some that I was sure I'd seen pictured in books.

"Do you like Picasso?" Erik asked.

I confessed my heart was really with Monet.

He smiled. "Ah, a romantic."

I thought only Paul Newman was allowed to have eyes that shade of blue. He had sandy hair turning to silver, a firm jaw; laugh lines crinkled the tanned skin. Around fifty, I'd say, certainly old enough to be my father if he'd had a wild teenage affair that produced a child.

Did he have children? Was there a Mrs. Lundstrom? I wished I'd paid more attention to the society column.

We ended up in a room that was bigger than some Cineplex theaters. The promised fire blazed cheerfully. On either side of the fireplace, wide windows looked out toward the sea, down to the lights of Laguna and Corona del Mar. Newport Beach twinkled in the rain-misted distance.

Three seven-foot sofas made a U in front of the fireplace. One each. I took a seat near the fire. The leather upholstery was butter-soft, comfortable as a bedroom slipper. Charlie sat across from me while Erik asked what we would like to drink, mixed them and brought the glasses over on a tray along with salted nuts and some cocktail napkins. He handed me my vodka and tonic and sat next to me.

I could feel his weight pushing down the cushions, tilting me very slightly toward him. I took a big swallow of vodka tonic and wiped my palms on a napkin.

After a few comments on the weather, Erik put down his glass and said, "How about we get the business stuff over with before dinner." He turned those blue, blue eyes on me. "Charlie tells me good things about you, Delilah. I have an opening here on my security staff."

He listed a dizzying salary and then added the perks. A car, an apartment here on the grounds, free travel on the company jet when there was space, generous time off to do the traveling.

"So," Erik said, "interested?"

Charlie watched me, rotund and silent. Funny, he didn't look a bit like a fairy godmother.

"Of course, sure," I said. "But—can I have some time to think about it?"

"Think? What's to think?" Charlie demanded.

"I do have a few other obligations." The insurance companies— no big deal. But Mike...

"The problem is I need somebody right away," Erik said.

"I could let you know tomorrow, the next day at the latest." As soon as the words were out, I wanted to retract them, say, How about moving in tonight? Jesus, what was wrong with me?

Erik smiled. "Okay, deal. Now let's go eat."

The houseman served dinner—broiled sea bass, potatoes, and broccoli. Plain food that sure didn't *taste* plain. Since I've yet to make an omelet that didn't turn into scrambled eggs, I had no idea what clever things the cook had done. We were just starting our raspberry frappe when Charlie was called away to the phone. He came back to say something had come up and he had to leave.

When I stood up to follow, Erik said, "Oh, stay, Delilah. Finish your dessert. I'll see that you get home."

"Well—"

"Better for me anyway," Charlie said. "I've got to go to the office."

He rushed off, leaving us to moosh around the ice in our long-stemmed glasses. Just the two of us, Erik and me, in that great big old dining room, sitting so close I could see the fine-grained texture of his skin and smell his clean, woodsy aftershave.

He put down his spoon, folded his napkin. "Coffee?"

"Yes, please."

"Be right back."

He went into the kitchen for a minute, returned and stood beside my chair. Obviously coffee would be served elsewhere. He took my arm and led me through the hallway. I had no idea where we were going and didn't really care.

He paused in front of a pair of double doors. "You'll have to promise to keep this a secret, okay?"

"Why?"

"You'll see. Promise?"

"Okay."

We went into a small entry. A suite, I realized. A bedroom suite. Although it was dark in there, I knew there was a big bed in the room off to the right. Lights glowed in the room on the left. The houseman, Ben, was there with a coffee tray. Another fireplace crackled. I could smell the wood burning, fresh coffee being poured.

Ben slipped out while I stood there, looking around. Only three paintings, but I didn't need an art book to recognize the shimmering impressionistic touch.

"So now you know," Erik said. "I'm a romantic too."

EIGHT

After all that we simply sat there and drank coffee and talked about the paintings, the changes in Orange County—he called it growth; I kept my opinion to myself—and me.

By the time he stood up and suggested it was time to have somebody drive me home, I'd told him that my mother died when I was five, my dad while I was in college, that I'd worked for the L.A.P.D., then married Jack, moved to Orange County and opened our detective agency and had been trying to make it on my own since Jack's death.

The thought did cross my mind—okay, more than once—that we'd progress from the personal to the intimate. On a trip to the bathroom to freshen up, I didn't see a thing either there or in the bedroom to indicate that a woman shared the suite. Of course, it was entirely possible that Mrs. Lundstrom had her own space down the hall.

I don't sleep around. In my opinion anybody who does these days is suicidal. Still, I wondered if he'd ask and if he did…well, he didn't.

"Be sure you let me know as soon as you make up your mind about the job," he said at the door as he helped me on with my raincoat.

The driver—Erik introduced him as Vincent—escorted me to the Rolls. I went reluctantly, a little disappointed. Riding down the narrow asphalt road, I began thinking about Erik's questions. Skillful, the way he'd drawn me out. I didn't like it much. Maybe I was a little embarrassed. Erik had been conducting a job interview. Never mind what I'd been doing.

Back at my office, I changed, put on pajamas and a robe, unrolled the sleeping bag, took my toothbrush down to the ladies' room. Erik's bathroom had been bigger than my entire office, and had its own built-in Jacuzzi. I trudged back to my sleeping bag, wondering how soon I could wrap up the Morales case.

Wondering just when it had become a *case.*

Was there really a possibility that Mr. Collins had been murdered? And if he had, who the hell was going to believe it? I didn't know Matt well enough to predict his reaction, but Lieutenant Brady was another matter. I had a feeling he rated me, on a scale of competence and logic, somewhere between Marie Antoinette and Edith Bunker.

Well, Mike had an attorney, didn't he? Matt would have no trouble taking my story apart on the witness stand. Maybe that would be enough to plant a reasonable doubt in the minds of a jury.

Yeah, maybe.

It was only ten forty-five, but I was tired and wanted to get an early start the next day. I switched off the light and was just zipping up the sleeping bag when the phone rang.

"So you're finally back," Rita said.

She had messages from Charlie and Matthew Scott.

Call me anytime before eleven, Matt had said.

He answered right away. "Just wanted to check in with you. Anything?"

I summed up the day's events, leaving out only Lucy Taylor's shopping habits and my evening with Erik and Charlie. I finished up by telling him about the shoe.

"Murder?" He didn't sound convinced. "I guess it's a possibility. But I'll need a lot more than a clean Florsheim to get past Devaney."

Tom Devaney, the district attorney, was young, aggressive and headed for a record conviction count. "You've got me," I said. "I'll testify to my doubts."

"Yeah, should be very convincing after you've told them that you identified the vehicle, that Mike almost ran you down, and then left the scene. And there's something else. Forensics identified a tire mark on Collins's raincoat. Guess what it matched?"

"Damn," I said. "What about the autopsy? Did you get a final report?"

He nodded. "Mr. Collins may very well have been alive when Mike ran over him. If he was dead, it wasn't for long. No *livor mortis*."

With no pooling of blood there was nothing to indicate he'd lain there after he died.

"How's Mike taking all this?" I asked.

"About how you'd expect. Sullen, bitter. Everybody's the enemy. He'll make a wonderful impression on a jury."

"You've decided to let it go to trial then? No plea bargaining?"

"I put out a feeler to the D.A.'s office. I had to. But the answer was loud and clear: no deals."

"They're going to make an example out of him."

"Looks that way." He paused, then said, "Listen, it's not all that late. How about a nightcap and we'll kick it around?"

"Well—"

"I'll meet you somewhere. Or you can come here."

A long time since I'd met an attractive man and now I'd met two. I wondered if he had a nice bathroom.

"I think I'd better take a pass," I said. "Some other time?"

"Sure." He sounded disappointed. "You are going to keep digging into Collins's death?"

I said I would and that I'd keep him informed.

I debated about calling Charlie and decided it was too late. Then the phone rang. Charlie.

"You just caught me," I said. "I had a few things to catch up on here so—"

"Oh, can it," he growled. "How'd it go with Erik?"

"It went fine. I told him I'd let him know in a day or two."

"Jesus Christ, Delilah, are you outta your mind? You're sleeping in your office and slinging hash to make ends meet. How can you pass this up?"

I'd been asking myself the same question. Still, I wondered why Charlie cared so much.

"If this is for old time's sake, Charlie, I think you and Jack are even now."

"Jack...yeah, well, I wasn't really thinking about Jack." An awkward pause. "Look, Delilah, this is a good deal for you, otherwise— sorry if I pushed."

Very strained. Weird. After I hung up and was trying to get comfortable on the hard floor, it hit me. Maybe that old obligation between Charlie and Jack had been settled long ago. Maybe Charlie was doing this for *me*. I usually just thought of him as kind of a walking IBM PC. But he had been married once. I suppose he'd been in love or at least had experienced lust. *Charlie?*

Lord...

I slept badly and was awake at five, stiff and miserable. Rather than bug my friends, I decided to go down to the Y for a shower. But first I made some coffee and drank it, staring out at the dark sullen skies.

If I really hustled, maybe I could finish with the doctors early and get on with the interviews—Ken Jacobs, Warren Kurtz, and most important, Amy Ferguson at Greenspace. Maybe if I was lucky, I could wrap things up, call Erik Lundstrom late today, and move in tonight. I didn't really believe it, but it was nice to think about all the same.

Still early when I got back from the Y. I had picked up an Egg McMuffin so I ate it at my desk while I did a little paperwork for the insurance companies and laid out the day's itinerary. As soon as possible, I called Collins Electronics. Warren wasn't in yet but I had his secretary put me down for an appointment at two-thirty.

The Greenspace number didn't answer. I kept trying it all morning in between sessions in doctors' waiting rooms.

I'd planned the last stop near South Coast Plaza. Since it was one o'clock, everybody in the medical office wanted to go to lunch, so I got out fast and went over to the shopping center.

South Coast Plaza had started out as a typical suburban mall, anchored by Sears and May Company. As a pleasant variation, there was a restored carousel in the middle, offering rides on the brightly painted horses for ten cents. Now the mall has gone upscale, kind of a Rodeo Drive South. If it's not the biggest in the country, it's close enough.

Lunch first, I decided, and headed for Vie de France for onion soup and fresh-baked bread. On the way, I took a quick look at the mall directory. There was a shop simply called Jacobs that sounded a likely bet.

I sat at a table in the mall concourse beneath banks of greenery, full-grown fan palms and weeping fig trees, people-watching. A definite international flavor in South Coast, with Arabic turbans and Indian saris mixed in with the California casual. After I finished the basket of bread and three cups of coffee, I went to find out what kind of shop Jacobs was and if Ken was the proprietor.

A small side window display featured a diamond necklace against black velvet. Discreet lettering gold-leafed on the glass read: Jacobs. Fine Jewelry. Investment Coins.

Most of the stores had sliding windows that opened up during shopping hours, but Jacobs was like an ordinary store with a front door. I'd bet it also had a full security system.

It was easy to understand why. No magpie clutter of watches, rings, and necklaces here. The locked cases displayed just a few spare arrangements of beautifully elegant, very expensive pieces and a selection of gold coins, the familiar Krugerrand and a variety of other specie.

Inside, the shop had pale-gray, silky wallpaper and plush gray carpets. A chime sounded as I opened the door. Two people sat at a desk behind the counter. I recognized the girl. It was Carolyn.

She said, "Miss West," in a startled voice at the same time the man stood up, smiled, and said, "May I help you?"

She joined him at the counter. "Daddy, this is Miss West. I told you about her, remember?"

His smile became slightly rigid, then slipped away. "Yes, of course. I'm Ken Jacobs, Miss West. It's *Delilah* West, isn't it?"

"Yes, it is."

"I see. Well—please. Come in. Sorry I missed you at the house yesterday." He fumbled with the latch on a hinged section of the counter.

Carolyn quickly did it for him, stage-managing him back into his chair and seating me on the other side while she perched on the edge beside her father. The desk was Shaker style, its glowing wood littered with envelopes and an open accounts journal.

Ken closed the book, began gathering up the mail. "How about something—tea? Carolyn, would you—"

"Oh, no thanks," I said. "I just had lunch."

"Is it that late already?"

"Daddy, didn't you eat yet?" Carolyn said. "I bet you skipped breakfast too."

"Oh, I'm fine." He wasn't. There were purple shadows under his eyes. His large, soft body had a slack look and the navy suit hung loosely as though he'd lost weight.

"If you don't take care of yourself, you're going to get sick," Carolyn said.

"Okay, mother hen. Go get something for me, all right?"

"Well…" She glanced at me. She didn't want to leave us alone for some reason.

"Please, darling," he said.

She agreed reluctantly. "What would you like?"

"Anything. Surprise me."

After she left, he turned to me. His eyes were the same shade of china blue as Carolyn's, the whites bloodshot. "Miss West, I have to talk to you. I heard something yesterday and if you could—clear it up for me…"

"What did you hear?"

"That you went—I mean, I think you went to see Lucy Taylor." He took out cigarettes and a gold lighter. His hands shook, but a lungful of smoke had a calming effect. "Lucy thought I should know that somebody talked to her about an insurance policy. A Miss Ames—Delilah Ames. The name and her description and now, meeting you…"

So the cat was out of the bag. I could deny it, of course, but what good would that do?

"You're right," I said. "I did go to see Mrs. Taylor. I was afraid she wouldn't talk to me if she knew I was a private investigator."

"But why did you want to talk to her?"

I debated. I could make something up, try to put him off. Or I could be blunt and see what the shock value got me.

"I'm trying to trace your father-in-law's movements the night he died. To be frank, I'm not sure his death was a simple hit and run."

"But then—what? You think Joe fell? Or had a heart attack maybe?"

"Not according to the autopsy."

"Then I don't see—what else could've happened?" He stared at me. "You don't think—that somebody *did* something—"

"It's a possibility."

"But you were there. You saw the Morales boy. You reported it to the police."

Without going into details, I told him about my meetings with Arlene Simpson and her son, about my growing doubts as to Mike's guilt.

"Well, the boy would say that, wouldn't he?" Ken stubbed out his cigarette and lit another. "He'd make up a story—do anything to get out of jail."

"He might," I admitted. "But I think he's telling the truth."

"Then you're working for them—the boy and his mother—trying to prove he's innocent?"

"Not exactly," I said, but that was no longer true so I amended, "Yes, I guess I am."

"Good God. Did you tell my wife about this?"

"No. When I went to see her, I didn't know myself."

"It's impossible." He shook his head. "Murder. That means somebody—but who? Do you have any clues? Suspects? What do the police say?"

"At this point, I don't have enough to go to the police. I was hoping you'd help me, Mr. Jacobs."

"Make it Ken, please." He tapped ashes into an ashtray, looking unhappy and distracted. "I don't see how I could. Things are bad enough right now. I don't think Pam could stand any more."

"But suppose I'm right. Don't you want the murderer found?"

"Of course, but what can I do to help you?"

"For starters, you can tell me about Mr. Collins's relationship with Warren Kurtz."

"Warren?" he said, startled. "What do you mean? Their business relationship?"

It seemed like a good place to start. Kurtz had stepped in to replace Joe Collins. I asked if there was any resentment on the old man's part.

"I don't really know. Joe wasn't pushed into selling. He just wanted to retire. Maybe he did have a hard time letting go, adjusting. They seemed to get along okay, at least on a professional level."

"What about a personal one?"

His hands moved around like large, helpless birds, crushing out his cigarette, disturbing the neat stacks of envelopes he'd arranged earlier. He finally said, "Carolyn told me that Warren was still there when you came to the house. So I guess you know—he and Pam— Joe was pretty upset about it. I told him not to worry. That Pam would come to her senses. That I loved her enough to wait and—"

He broke off and stared at me in horror. "My God, you don't suspect Warren?"

"A detective suspects everybody. How about you? Where were you that night?"

"Here. Working late." He looked even sicker. "Surely you don't think—I loved Joe."

"I have to ask. Was anybody here with you?"

"No—"

The door chime sounded and Carolyn came in with a large Styrofoam container. She looked from me to him and said firmly, "Now, Daddy, I want you to take this in back and have a nice quiet lunch. I'll watch the shop. You'll excuse him, won't you, Miss West?"

"I was just leaving."

"Wait a second," Ken said. "There was one more thing. Carolyn, honey, will you get that ready for me? Please?"

She hesitated, studying the two of us, before she went reluctantly through a door that opened into the back area. As soon as it closed behind her, Ken said, "Delilah, Joe's death has been terrible for Carolyn and Pam. Now this…can't you keep them out of it?"

"I don't know if that's possible."

"Can you try? Please. I promise I'll help you all I can."

I got out of answering because Carolyn came out with a determined look on her face and shooed him away. He gave me one last pleading look. I felt as though I'd taken up shooting bunny rabbits for a living.

As I stood up and started around the desk, I brushed against the stack of mail and it scattered on the floor. I knelt to pick it up. Bills. A lot of bills. Electricity. Telephone. Several loan companies. Some marked Second Notice. I finished restacking them on the desk as Carolyn came out.

"Is he all right?" I asked.

"I think I talked him into taking a nap after lunch. There's a cot in back. Poor Daddy. It's been an awful year for him. But they say bad things come in threes. I hope so, because he's had about all he can take."

Three? I figured Pam's relationship with Warren for one and Mr. Collins's death for two but—"What else happened to your father?"

"Oh, it's silly, I guess. I was thinking about the robbery here at the shop. The insurance covered it but still—it would count, wouldn't it? If you were superstitious?"

I'd done enough rabbit hunting for the day, so I murmured something I hoped sounded comforting and left the quiet store for the clamor of the mall.

NINE

Before I left South Coast Plaza, I tried Greenspace again. No luck. I double-checked with Information to make sure I had the right number. I did.

I put my money back in the pay phone and dialed my office. Rita said Charlie had called. So had Matt. And Arlene Simpson.

"That's all?"

"That's not enough?" Rita asked.

No time to call anybody back. I was running late. On the freeway up to Fullerton for my appointment with Warren Kurtz, I thought about Ken Jacobs. From the pile of bills, he owed money. A lot?

There had been a robbery at the shop.

And not a single customer had crossed the threshold while I was there, not even one who was "just looking."

So what the hell did all that mean? Probably that I was just naturally suspicious. Wouldn't it be funny if somebody at Greenspace had a perfectly reasonable explanation for how Mr. Collins left the meeting and wound up in the street without getting mud on his shoes?

Funny for whom? Not for Mike. Or his mother.

Face it. I was looking for an easy way out because I really was considering the offer from Erik. Of course, accepting the job meant closing my office. Was I ready to do that?

Maybe so. Maybe.

Traffic slowed to a crawl, so I got off the freeway and took to the side streets, arriving at the plant at two-forty-five. I went in an entrance gate where a uniformed guard checked my name off a list.

He sent me over to the executive offices housed in a one-story red brick building with some ivy and low-growing juniper and two big birds-of-paradise growing by the front door. I could see three more buildings in back, huge and functional, aluminum gray.

Inside, the building had the old solid feel of lathe and plaster walls and real wood moldings. The reception area had deep-pile camel carpeting and a lot of glass and chrome.

I got directions from the receptionist to Warren's private quarters, which rated its own spacious front office with a leggy blond secretary. She was going through some files. A man looked over her shoulder, leaning one hand on the desk.

The woman saw me and said, "Miss West?"

"Yes. Sorry I'm late. Traffic," I explained. Traffic was a very good excuse in Orange County these days.

"I'm afraid there was an emergency. Mr. Kurtz had to go over to the plant."

"Nothing serious, I hope."

"Some kind of production snafu," the man said. He straightened up and introduced himself as Bill Irwin, Warren's assistant.

Late twenties with a runner's body, lean and hard, inside his impeccably tailored tan suit. Dark hair with a *GQ* cut and a mustache, neatly trimmed. He assessed me with eyes the color and texture of chocolate pudding.

"Will Mr. Kurtz be back soon?" I asked.

"Shouldn't be too long." He glanced at his watch. "Tell you what. I'm due for a break. Why don't I buy you a cup of coffee! Warren will be back by then."

He didn't give me time to object. He strode around the desk and headed for the door, holding it open, saying to the secretary "Nancy, tell Warren, will you?" He waited, smiled. "Miss West?"

There was a distinct change of decor as we went down a labyrinth of corridors to the cafeteria. Things weren't exactly rundown, but the walls needed paint and the carpet was worn.

The coffee was good, though. While we sipped, he kept up a line of chit-chat. The terrible weather. Collins Electronics' reputation in the field of circuit boards. I nodded in all the right places.

Finally he gave me an open, engaging grin. "Should I keep going? I'm good at small talk."

"So I gathered."

"I recognized your name. Warren mentioned meeting you after the funeral, and I saw the newspaper report. I know it's none of my business, but I can't help wondering why you want to see Warren."

He was right, it wasn't any of his business. On the other hand, his curiosity gave me an opening. "A few things bother me about the way Mr. Collins died. So I'm asking some questions. How long have you worked here, Mr. Irwin?"

"Bill, please. I've been here four months."

"How well did you know Mr. Collins?"

"I only met him a few times. He used to visit the plant."

"On a regular basis?"

"No, he'd just drop by now and then. Probably had a lot of time on his hands after he retired."

"Did Warren mind the interruptions?"

"I don't know. Maybe. But Mr. Collins did found the company. Kind of like having a child. No matter what happens, it's still your baby."

And if you don't like what's happening to it, do you react the way a mother does when she protects her young?

"Somebody mentioned that Mr. Collins came into the office the afternoon just before he died," I said. "Did you see him?"

"No. I think I was over in the plant area most of that day. Nancy might know. Delilah—okay to call you Delilah?" Another engaging grin. His best feature and he knew it.

"Sure."

"Isn't it kind of odd? You were the eyewitness to the hit and run. If you saw it—you did see it?"

I hadn't, not exactly, so I hesitated before I said, "Yes, of course," and he picked up on it.

"But not really?" he asked softly.

I glanced at my watch: three-fifteen. "I think I'll check on Warren, see if he's back. I have another stop to make."

He tagged along. "Sorry if I'm nosy, Delilah. Tell the truth, the whole private eye thing fascinates me. Spenser, Travis McGee, Jim Rockford, Simon and Simon. How about having a drink with me tonight? I'd love to hear about your work."

Three attractive men now and this one a groupie. The tide really had turned.

"Gee, I'd like to but I'm afraid I'm busy," I said.

"Can I call you?"

"I'm in the phone book."

At Warren's suite, he held the door for me. Inside, Nancy was just coming out of Warren's office. She tilted an eyebrow at Bill, some kind of code, translated when Warren growled from the other room, "And send Irwin in here as soon as he gets back."

Bill winked at me and hurried off. Nancy assured me it would just be a few minutes. I sat down to wait. Spread on a coffee table were several copies of a slickly printed, magazine-size brochure titled: "The Collins Story." I picked one up.

Everything you ever wanted to know about electronic circuit boards, from the basic design and layout through various stages of putting the design on the board by a photographic process and chemically etching the circuit patterns, to wiring in the components. A double-page spread gave a montage of the products that used the boards: all sizes of computers, television sets, electronic games, timers that made coffee and operated automated burglar alarm systems.

The brochure did an excellent job of presenting the subject in layman's terms. It also painted a glowing picture of Collins Electronics' future. I wondered why I felt that I was getting a hard sell.

The door to Warren's office opened and Bill Irwin walked out with Warren close behind.

"I want that sales report as soon as you have it," Warren said. "Miss West? Come in please."

The request was brusque and there was a grim set to his mouth. No warm smiles today or dulcet tones. Bill gave me a sympathetic look as we passed each other.

"Sorry I was late," I said as Warren closed the door and went around his desk to sit, facing me.

He was all business, from his dark-blue herringbone suit to the coldness in his voice. "This won't take long, Miss West. I spoke with Lieutenant Brady earlier this afternoon. He assured me you won't be harassing any of us anymore."

"I saw you once at the Jacobses'. I made an appointment to see you today. How do you get harassment from that?"

"I'm not talking about myself. Look, Pam called me late yesterday, very upset."

It seems Pam had gone over to the retirement hotel to start packing up her father's things, and Mrs. Beardsley had mentioned that an insurance investigator from California Life had been around asking questions. Her father didn't have a policy with California Life. The description of this investigator sounded familiar, however. Pam didn't place it until awhile later when she spoke with Carolyn at the jewelry shop. Carolyn had told her mother that I had been there, talking to Ken.

"We don't know why you're snooping around, Miss West," Warren said. "But I can think of a few nasty possibilities and it's going to stop right now."

"Meaning?"

"Blackmail. Those supermarket scandal sheets pay pretty well, I understand."

"Mr. Kurtz, for your information I'm not making a dime from this investigation. As a matter of fact, I may lose out on a damn good job offer because of it."

"What investigation?"

"A possible homicide."

"You mean murder? Whose murder?" He stared at me. *"Joe's?* Are you *nuts?"*

"That seems to be the general consensus," I said. "And, listen, before you start telling me how much pain and suffering this is going to cause the Jacobs family, let me say I've heard it all from Ken. And I sympathize, I really do. But there's a boy in the Orange County Jail who's suffering too. He's not a nice, straight kid everybody can feel sorry for because he made one little mistake. He's a loser who looks like he beats up on little old ladies and steals their Social Security checks, and it's my testimony that's going to put him away. Problem is, I think for once this kid's probably telling the truth. So I don't really care if you like it or not. I'm going to be around asking questions. For instance, why was Mr. Collins here the day he died?"

"What?" I couldn't tell if his surprise was genuine or if he was stalling.

"He came to see you that afternoon. I want to know why."

"What on earth for? Are you accusing *me* of something?"

"Not exactly."

"You'd better not be. Not unless you have some damn good evidence to back up your accusations."

"Evidence?" I shrugged. "I'm still working on motive. Take you for example. I'm just brainstorming here, of course, but I'd guess something to do with the business. Or maybe Mr. Collins didn't like your breaking up his daughter's marriage. Maybe he thought of some way to stop you from seeing her."

"Don't be ridiculous. The marriage was in trouble for a long time and Joe knew it. As for anything to do with Collins Electronics, that's nonsense."

"Is it? Then tell me what you and Joe talked about."

"None of your damned business," he said. He got up and strode around the desk, threw open the door.

Bill Irwin was standing beside Nancy's desk, file folders in hand. They both had the look of the avidly curious getting an earful.

"Are those the sales figures?" Warren asked. "Let's get to it."

I heard the door slam as I left the suite. I felt like slamming a few doors myself. Mostly, though, I was mad at myself. I'd lost it in there. Blown my cool. Maybe Charlie had been right after that fiasco at May Company. Maybe I should consider another line of work.

TEN

Harry was waiting at the back door of my office building, watching for my car. "I sure am glad you got back before I had to leave, Miz West. I seen this guy hanging around today, real nasty-looking customer. Wanted to warn you to keep your eyes open tonight—in case you're working late, I mean."

"Thanks, Harry. I'll do that."

"Got a good description of him right here." He whipped out a piece of yellow paper and thrust it at me.

An advertising flyer for Kay Chong's Chinese, torn in half, Harry's crabbed script on the back.

"Keep it," I said. "If you see him again, call the cops."

I didn't mean for it to come out so snappish, but I wasn't in the mood to cater to the old guy just then. So I stomped off upstairs, gave my door a nice satisfying slam, and plopped down in my comfortable wingback.

I'd set off this morning expecting to accomplish enough to start winding down this case, and what did I have? Ken Jacobs's financial problems. A possibility of some kind of business friction between Warren Kurtz and Joe Collins. Still no contact with Greenspace to find out who saw the old man last.

Back up. You're supposed to be a detective here. The most important question in any murder investigation is always: Who has a motive? Of course the reason I was floundering around was I still didn't know for sure if Mr. Collins had been murdered. But assume he had. Lots of motives for killing somebody. Heading the list is money, hatred, passion.

Just because he was seventy-two, that didn't rule out affairs of the heart, but it definitely put them in the number-three spot. And he could've made lots of enemies over the years. Even though I hadn't uncovered any, that kind of hate runs cold and deep. As for money, I needed to know first if there was any and, second, who was going to get it.

I called Charlie Colfax.

"Nice of you to fit me into your busy schedule," he said after I ran the gamut of secretaries. "You talk to Erik yet?"

"No, I just got in."

"You finish poking around in Collins's death?"

"I'm trying to wrap it up, but I could use a favor, Charlie."

"What else is new?"

"I can do the digging on my own. It'll just take longer."

"Okay, okay. What do you need?"

I told him I'd like Collins's financial status and the details of the will. Something on Ken Jacobs's shop. Background checks on both Ken and Pamela, Warren Kurtz, and—a long shot—Bill Irwin.

"Who was that last one?" Charlie asked.

I repeated the name and told him he worked for Warren.

"I guess I can't talk you out of this?"

"No, Charlie."

"All right, I'll get back to you."

With the Colfax computers, I figured that shouldn't take too long. Trouble was, he probably agreed only so I would finish up with the case and go to work for Erik. I just wished I knew why my career was suddenly so important to him.

The phone rang.

"Well, at last," Rita said. "Miss Popularity. Is there a possibility that somewhere on this list of people dying to speak to you lurks a paying customer?"

"Maybe. Who called?"

"Likely prospects first." She reeled off Charlie, Matt, Arlene, one of my insurance clients, and Erik Lundstrom. "Not *the* Erik Lundstrom?"

"The very one. Did he leave a message?"

"Wow! I'm impressed. He just said to remind you to call him soon."

Not an invitation to come up and look at his Monets, but it was something.

"Also, Jorge Sanchez called," Rita said. "Roughly translated, I think he said they were getting together a poker game tonight. And now for the bad news. A Lieutenant Brady wants to see you A.S.A.P. What did you do?"

"It's a long story."

"How about telling us over dinner? I'll even throw in a bubble bath."

I couldn't face one of Farley's meals so I begged off. Brady would just want to rag on me because of Warren's call. I didn't need to hear it on an empty stomach. Jorge's call reminded me I never had tracked down Mr. Collins's poker-playing friends. Maybe later. It had been a long time since the soup and French bread.

I checked the larder. Nothing in my lower desk drawer but a jar of Fisher's unsalted peanuts and two granola bars. My cash was down to five dollars and twenty-three cents.

Maybe they'd have a dinner special at Al's Diner.

I called to see if Arlene was working, and then I called Matt to ask if he wanted to meet me there. With any luck he might even pick up the check.

The diner was noisy and warm, redolent with the smell of frying onions. Arlene seated me in a booth and hovered anxiously. "Have you found out anything at all, Miss West?"

A tough choice. I could tell her my suspicions and get her hopes up, then have to crush them later if Mr. Collins really had died beneath the wheels of Mike's car.

"Nothing concrete," I said. "But I'm working on a few leads."

"I'm not trying to push you. It means so much that you're willing to help us." She handed me a menu. Her nails were chewed down to the cuticle. "It's just—thinking about Mike in that jail—"

"As soon as I come up with something for sure, I'll let you know," I said.

Matt came in and headed over. He'd seen Mike that afternoon and could reassure Arlene that her son was holding up all right.

After she went off to get coffee for us, I asked, "Is he really okay?"

"Well, he's putting on a good show. How's the investigation going?"

I told him about my visit to Ken Jacobs's shop and to Collins Electronics, my report broken by Arlene's trips back and forth.

"Not much to go on," he said when I finished. "Did you ever reach anybody from Greenspace?"

I shook my head. "What do you know about the organization?"

"Not a lot. They keep a low profile, but they've taken on a couple of big corporations and won, so I'll bet there's big bucks involved."

"You'd think they'd use some of it to staff an office. If I ever get in touch with them, maybe I can find out exactly when Mr. Collins left the meeting in the park and if he left alone. Or at least find out who was at the meeting and talk to them."

Arlene came back for our order. Meatloaf was the only entree that fit my budget. I settled for a large bowl of beef and vegetable soup. I could pick up a few bucks tonight at the poker game and I still had money coming from the insurance companies, but that wasn't enough to keep me going. Sooner or later I'd have to go back to work at Mom's just to eat.

Or accept Erik Lundstrom's offer.

I sighed.

"What?" Matt asked.

"I'm not sure how much more time I can give to this case, Matt. I've been offered a job and the problem is, I have to make a quick decision."

He studied me over his coffee. "You're considering it seriously."

"I'd be a fool not to. I'm getting some background material on the Jacobses and Warren Kurtz and I'll spend tomorrow tracking down the Greenspace people, but after that—"

Arlene hustled over with the food, that terrible anxious, eager-to-please look on her face. My appetite vanished.

"I take it you haven't told Arlene," Matt said when she left us alone.

From the way he said it and the look on his face, I could see his opinion of me had dropped several notches. Well, he wasn't the one who was living in his office and eating stale granola bars.

"She understood going in that this was a long shot."

"Uh-huh."

We ate in polite silence and I got out of there as quickly as I could. He didn't offer to pick up the check, but Arlene did. I refused, paying my own way and leaving a generous tip.

The poker game wouldn't start until almost eleven. I wanted to go back to my office to change clothes, but I didn't want to sit there for two hours, so I took a swing over to Newport and headed south.

I passed the road heading up to Erik's house and glimpsed the lights high in the hills. I could be up there, part of that exclusive little haven. Just say the word, Delilah.

Defeat. Surrender. Failure.

What was wrong with thinking of it as a fresh start?

South of Laguna, rain splattered my windshield and I had to turn on the wipers. Through the smeary glass I could see the bare wood bones of the latest housing development being built off to the right.

To drive down the coast is to know how life constantly changes. A few years ago the cliffs north of Dana Point had been barren, deserted. Jack had died out there on a rainy night just like this, died in my arms from a gunshot wound, his blood pumping out to soak into the cold, wet earth. Eventually I had learned to live with the pain of losing Jack. To cope. Compartmentalize. And now the cliffs are covered with condos and townhomes and the bland sprawl of the Ritz-Carlton Hotel.

Things change. Life goes on.

I swung around and got on the freeway. Traffic was light. I'd make it back to my office in half an hour. Plenty of time to call Erik Lundstrom before I left for the game.

I parked over in the far corner behind my office building where there's a cement block wall and some spindly bushes so my car wouldn't be visible from the street. No sense raising the curiosity of a passing patrol car. The rain had turned to a fine mist. I pulled my coat tighter and shivered.

One of the lights in the lot was out, the other dirty and dim. Rain trickled down my collar, snaking coldly down my spine. There was a light on inside the lobby—at least a twenty-five watter. Big help. The dumpster loomed against the wall. I could smell the rancid, foul odor.

Something rustled in the bushes. A cat—or maybe the guy Harry had said was hanging around? I scanned the darkness, all my senses revving up. I own a gun, but it was upstairs, locked in my desk. My car keys were still in my hand. I fumbled them into place, positioning the keys between my fingers, not quite ready when a dark shape separated from the building and lunged at me.

I lashed out and heard a grunt of pain, but I was already falling. My head slammed into the wet asphalt and millions of little colored starbursts exploded in my skull.

I was facedown in a puddle of oily water, but before I could worry about drowning, fingers tangled in my hair and yanked me up. Elbows clamped me against a bony chest. Tears sprang from my eyes, and my nose leaked blood. I could taste it.

He was squatting or kneeling beside me. I couldn't see him, but there was a coarse beard against my cheek and something cold and sharp against my throat.

"That's a knife," he said. "You feel it? That's fuckin' *real*. You give me any shit, I'll use it, Delilah. I mean like I'll really fuckin' *stick* you."

"Right," I croaked. "Okay."

"You already hurt my face, like I got this fuckin' big cut and I'm bleedin' and you better *believe* I ain't gonna let you hurt me again."

"Just—tell me—what you want. Money? My purse—over there—"

With one dollar and fifty-seven cents in it. But all I wanted was to distract him.

"Don't be so fuckin' stupid." He gave my hair another vicious yank. "Get up and like do it real slow and easy. We're goin' inside where it ain't so fuckin' cold and wet and have a little talk."

He got up, pulling me with him, releasing my arms—for all the good it did me. The knife was still against my carotid artery, razor sharp.

"Sure," I said. "Okay. But listen, the building's locked. And my keys are in my purse."

He hesitated. Dithered is a better word. I could smell his high ripe sweat.

"All right," he said. "Shit. Where is the fuckin' thing?"

We both saw it just in the edge of murky light spilling from the lobby. He began hauling me over. He was either going to have to let me unlock the door or he'd have to let go my hair to do it himself. Either way…an instant, that's all I needed. A split second—

The lobby door banged open and Harry barreled out, yelling "I got him, I got him," pipe wrench in hand.

The man's arm tightened and the knife dug into my skin. I pulled away, sure the artery was severed and pumping blood, grabbed my throat to hold the artery closed, realized that I wasn't cut and that I was free. The man had released me because Harry was plunging straight at him.

No time to yell a warning. Light glinted on the knife. Then Harry gave a hoarse bleat of pain and slumped, grabbing at the man and buckling at the knees.

The man stared at me over Harry's upturned face. Unarmed now because the knife was in Harry's chest. But all he had to do was pull it out and—

I moved fast, inside the door Harry had left open. Safe inside while Harry collapsed on the wet asphalt.

ELEVEN

I slammed the door and leaned against it, holding it shut. My breath frosted the glass so that the man who crouched over Harry looked like some long, skinny monster floating upright in an aquarium.

Since I didn't have my keys, I couldn't lock myself in. I *could* run upstairs, break the frosted window of my office door, and get to my gun...which was locked in my desk and, anyway, the damn thing wasn't loaded.

Jesus, Jesus...

I stood there and he stood there, neither of us capable of making a decision. Then he knelt beside Harry for a second. When he got up, light glinted briefly on the knife in his hand before he ran off into the darkness.

I retreated inside to a pay phone and dialed 911, police emergency, asking for the paramedics, not wasting time on supplying the address because the computer would lock in automatically.

That done, I ran outside, straining to see into the blackness. The pipe wrench lay where Harry had dropped it. I picked it up, just in case the knife-wielder planned a return visit, and knelt down by the old man. At least he was alive. I could hear his liquidy breathing.

He lay on his side with his knees drawn up. The front of his T-shirt was bloody, a dark purple in the sickly light. I took off my raincoat and put it over him, trying not to think of that other January night five years ago.

"Harry—my God, Harry, what were you doing here?"

He should've been home by now, wherever home was, watching TV, having a beer. Stupid, idiotic, crazy old man...

"Miz—West—"

"Shh, lie still. The paramedics are coming."

"Told you—that guy—"

"I know you did."

"Wanted—be sure—you—okay—"

"I'm fine. I'm just fine. Now, be quiet. Don't talk."

I heard sirens and told Harry I was going to leave him for a second. No way was I going to circle the building through the dark parking lot. I cut through the lobby instead and went out the front entrance to wave to the paramedics.

A black and white arrived right behind them. The cops listened to my capsule account and took off on a foot search while the medics worked on Harry.

They packed the wound, got him on a stretcher and covered up, hung an I.V. One of them handed me back my raincoat. By then I was soaked, my teeth chattering, but I stood there, holding the bloodstained garment, unwilling to put it on.

"Hurts," Harry mumbled. "Bad—how bad?"

"Don't worry, sir," the medic said. "We're taking you to the hospital."

"Hate—hospitals. Die—in hospitals—Miz West?"

"I'm right here, Harry."

"Don't—go 'way—"

One of the cops came back just as Harry was being loaded into the ambulance. "No sign of him. My partner's calling it in. Why don't we get outta the rain and get your statement."

Harry was still babbling, calling my name.

I grabbed my purse and my keys. "You want a statement, you can come to the hospital," I said and climbed in beside Harry.

The cop didn't like it, but the ambulance was already rolling. I crouched beside the stretcher, gripping Harry's hand, trying to read the medic's face.

"Is he going to be all right?"

"I'm afraid you'll have to ask the doctor."

"But you must have some idea."

"Depends on how much internal damage there is. Does he have a history of heart disease? Any allergies to medication?"

I didn't know. I knew nothing about him. He was just an old man who cleaned the floors and fixed the plumbing. A damned nuisance. A pest.

At the hospital there was another barrage of questions after Harry was taken into the emergency room. Insurance? Relatives? Next of kin? I kept shaking my head.

"Does he have any kind of insurance at all?"

That seemed to be the single most important question. I gave them the name of the building management company, but nobody was answering the company's phone this time of night. Harry's wallet yielded a faded Social Security card, an old picture of a heavier younger Harry with a plump red-haired woman, a few crumpled bills, an old Dear Abby column with the Alcoholics Anonymous creed. No insurance card.

The clerk frowned at her computer screen. "You ought to've told the paramedics so they could've taken him to County. We don't have any wards here."

"You have doctors, don't you?"

"You don't seem to understand. If he's an indigent—"

"How can he be an indigent? He has a job."

"But if he doesn't have insurance—"

Cold air blasted down from a vent. Forty degrees outside, but in here the air-conditioning was on. My teeth began chattering again.

"Is there anyplace I can get a cup of coffee?"

"The cafeteria's closed. Now about these forms—"

"Shove your forms."

I left her with her mouth hanging open and went in search of a nurse. Harry was on his way to surgery. She said the operation might take hours. Why didn't I go on home? I said I'd wait and she promised to have them call down from O.R.

In the waiting room, the patrolman had arrived and was talking to the clerk. She gestured toward me, shooting me a vindictive smile, delighted to sic the police on me.

The cop introduced himself as Sergeant Denbo. We sat in the icy lounge while I told him about the attack. I gave him as good a description as I could, but that wasn't much. I was exhausted, my mind as numb as my feet.

The phone rang several times. The clerk answered it, pointedly ignoring me.

"You hear anything yet about Mr. Polk?" Denbo asked.

"Not yet." Maybe never if the woman at the desk could help it.

"Well, they got good doctors here. He's in good hands." He shifted on the couch. "About tonight—you work this late often?"

"Pretty often."

He scratched more notes. "I don't have your home address."

I gave him Rita's.

"Now exactly where did you say the assailant was when you first noticed him?"

I told him about the dark parking lot, the knife, the way Harry rushed out, feeling removed, as though I was repeating gossip. Denbo scrawled notes, then finally closed his book and said I should come down tomorrow to sign a statement and look at some mug shots. "Maybe we'll get lucky." He stood up to go.

"Sergeant Denbo? Do you know—what happens if Harry hasn't got insurance?"

"They'll send him to County as soon as they can. That's a good hospital too," he assured me.

Maybe it was. I huddled on the couch after he left, thinking that no matter how good it was, the place was bound to be crowded and impersonal and I didn't want Harry shipped off there.

I found a pay phone. Probably way too late to call Erik Lundstrom, but I dialed the number anyway. He answered promptly.

"Is the job still open?" I asked.

"Yes."

"I'll take it."

"Well—wonderful."

"Just one thing—I need to use your name tonight, as an employment reference. Is that all right? I mean, I know there's paperwork and that won't be done right away, but—"

"Delilah, what's wrong?"

"A friend of mine was hurt. He's in the hospital."

"Which hospital? Where are you?"

I told him.

"I'll be right there."

Ten minutes later he walked in the door. Which seemed physically impossible until he explained he had just been leaving the Orange County Performing Arts Center and took my call in his Rolls. He wore a tux with a pleated shirt and a gray cummerbund, elegantly, nonchalantly handsome. The clerk stared, dazzled.

One look at me and Erik took off his jacket and draped it over my shoulders, sent the clerk scurrying for coffee and a blanket. He listened to my explanation without interruption, then took charge while I luxuriated in the taste of the coffee, the feel of the blanket around my knees, in the spectacle of the system being brought to heel by power and money.

Of course money couldn't do a hell of a lot for Harry just then up on that operating table, and it couldn't make the time go faster. Erik sat with me, waiting, until the doctor came to tell us that Harry had survived the operation and was in Intensive Care. Now only time would tell.

I didn't know how tired I was until I stood up and walked outside to the Rolls. Simply picking up my feet and putting them down took enormous concentration, and I had a hard time aiming my body at the car door.

"Sorry—"

"We'd better get you home," Erik said.

Home...

"Have to go to my office." The Rolls's interior was a warm, leather-scented cocoon. I leaned back, my eyelids slipping closed. "Pick up my car..."

"I don't think so." Erik put his arm around me. "Not tonight."

I snuggled into the hollow of his shoulder and drifted off, lulled by the hum of the engine and the *whish* of tires on wet pavement. The thought winged through my head that I didn't know where we were going and that I didn't really care.

When we stopped, I woke up, disoriented and groggy, just long enough to realize I was being led into Erik's house. Then there was a gap while I literally slept on my feet, and the next thing I knew I was being tucked into a big, warm crisp-sheeted bed.

"Erik?"

His fingers brushed my hair back from my face, lingered on my cheek. "Go to sleep."

"Erik? Is there a Mrs. Lundstrom?"

A hell of a time to doze off, but I did...and woke up sometime later to the sound of rain hissing on the window, expecting him next to me. Disappointed because I was alone. Burrowing back under the covers, I remembered everything, all of it unreeling in a split second, every intimate, brutal detail, and I knew the attack couldn't have been a simple mugging or attempted rape.

The man in the parking lot had known my name.

TWELVE

When I awakened the next morning, I found my clothes, cleaned, pressed, and folded, on a chair beside the bed. Which led to the interesting question of who had removed them the night before. There was also a white terry-cloth robe handy. I got up, put it on, and discovered first the bathroom and then thermal servers of juice and coffee on a tray beside the telephone.

Sipping coffee, I decided this was a guest room, not the digs I'd be living in when I started working here. There was pale-blue moire wallpaper and antique furniture, old wood lovingly polished, an overstuffed loveseat in a satiny print.

I sat on the edge of the bed and pushed buttons on the phone until I got an outside line. Information gave me the number for the hospital. The hospital told me Harry was still in critical condition.

At least he'd made it through the night.

I took my coffee and went over to pull the drapes and looked out toward Laguna. The sky was slate gray. A big live oak dripped outside the window. Just beyond, the ground sloped away, down to a wild, wooded canyon.

While I stood there, Erik walked up from the canyon. A big golden Labrador trotted beside him. Erik wore jeans and an old leather jacket. His head was bare. He moved quickly and easily, stopping to throw a stick for the dog.

I remembered what I'd asked him last night. *Is there a Mrs. Lundstrom?* I wished I'd stayed awake long enough to hear his answer.

Quickly I stepped back before he saw me and closed the drapes. In the bathroom after a long, hot shower, I wrapped myself in a plush slate-blue bath sheet and thought how easy it would be to get used to this kind of luxury. How nice to have somebody like Erik come to your rescue.

Personally I'd always believed that comes the crunch, the only person you can count on is yourself, but then I'd never had a lot of white knights standing by.

I got dressed and went out in the hall to find a maid hovering there. She mentioned breakfast and guided me down the corridors toward the smell of coffee and bacon. Had Erik waited to eat with me?

The breakfast room was just off the kitchen, small, informal. Sliding doors opened onto a Mexican tiled patio and when the fog cleared, there would be a multimillion-dollar view of the sea. Somebody sat at a round oak table. Not Erik. Charlie.

"Delilah, hell of a thing last night." He was reading the paper. The page three headline said: *Santa Ana Man Stabbed by Mugger.* "Too bad it took something like this to make you come to your senses."

"Yes," I said. "Too bad."

He took an orange from a centerpiece basket and cut it open. The inside was bright red. Even the juice flowed the color of blood.

"Want some?" he said.

"No, thanks."

The houseman came in with a plate of sliced melon, poured me coffee, and asked what I'd like to eat. When he went back in the kitchen with my order for scrambled eggs and bacon, I heard Erik's voice and the dog's deep woof.

Erik came to the door to say good morning and that he'd be in as soon as he took care of Astrid.

"Feeds that dog himself," Charlie said. "Brushes her. Sat up the whole damn night once when she got bit by a coyote."

"Is there a Mrs. Lundstrom?"

"Not now. There've been two." Charlie ate an orange segment and eyed me speculatively.

I busied myself with the cantaloupe. "Did you get those reports for me?"

"You're not serious? Erik said you'd accepted the job with him."

"I won't be working twenty-four hours a day. Do you have the information or not?"

"Yeah, I got it." His briefcase was on the floor by his chair. He dug in it and took out some computer printouts. "You're going to run yourself ragged and maybe screw up this job, and then what? Go back to slinging hash and fighting off muggers and rapists?"

"That's not how it was, Charlie. The guy last night knew me. Somebody's nervous. They want to scare me off."

"Oh, come on. You really believe that?"

"Yes."

It was obvious he didn't, but he gave me his report while I ate. Mr. Collins's will had been filed for probate. No surprises. Aside from a trust fund for Carolyn, the rest of his estate went to Pam.

"Anything on Collins Electronics?"

"Bought out by Penn Industries and they paid off Mr. Collins at the time of sale. Profits are down. Maybe they were looking for a tax write-off."

As for Warren Kurtz, he was barely holding his financial head above water. A rented townhouse, a company Mercedes, and a good chunk of his handsome salary going for alimony and child support. When he moved out from Baltimore to manage the company, his wife and two children stayed behind.

"Okay," I said. "What about Bill Irwin?"

"Nothing much. U.C.L.A., good credit history. Your average Yuppie."

Well, it had been a long shot. Charlie moved on to Ken Jacobs. If Warren was treading water, Ken was going down for the third time. He'd lost a bundle on the overbuilt commercial development market. The jewelry store was ready to fold.

I remembered what Carolyn had told me. "Did you come across anything about a robbery at his store?"

"Wait a second." He leafed through the fan-folded paper. "Yeah, here. A diamond bracelet, couple of rings, never recovered. Prime stuff. The insurance settlement was two hundred thousand." He looked up. "Any of this mean anything to you?"

"Not a whole lot," I admitted.

"That's because you're mining a dry hole," Charlie growled.

I tried to think of a good comeback, but just then Erik came in, bringing my breakfast himself. "I just got off the phone with the hospital," he said.

"Is Harry any better?"

"I'm afraid not. I told them to keep us posted, and I've alerted the staff."

"Thanks," I said, "for everything."

He didn't sit down. Instead Charlie used his napkin, stood up, and picked up his briefcase.

"I'm glad I could help," Erik said. "After breakfast, I've asked Vincent to show you your apartment. Then he can give you a hand moving your things in."

"Erik—I've got some things to take care of first. Can I move in tonight?"

He glanced at Charlie, then nodded. "Of course. I'll tell the gate to expect you this evening. Now, if you'll excuse us..."

They left and I sat there, feeling excluded and let down. Last night...had I misread Erik so completely? Face it. The man was just being kind, fatherly even. Not a comforting thought.

As soon as I finished my eggs, Vincent came in. I told him I was pushed for time so I'd take a pass on looking at the apartment. In the Rolls, we cruised through the last clots of rush-hour traffic back to Santa Ana. All I could think of was how much of a kick Harry would have gotten seeing me get out of that big white car.

Vincent slowed in front of my building but didn't stop. "Miss West, I think there's an unmarked police car across the street. Is that a problem?"

"A small one. Drop me around the block, will you?"

"Sure thing."

The parking lot for my building was separated from the one in back by the low cinder block wall. I cut through the lot, clambered over the wall, and went in the back way.

Upstairs in my office, I checked in with Rita.

"Jeez, Delilah, don't you ever think people might worry about you? Every time I pick up the paper, you just had another near miss."

"Sorry. It was a hell of an evening."

"You're telling me. All your friends were frantic. Especially Matthew Scott. Am I ever going to get to meet any of these guys?"

"It's business, Rita."

"Yeah, sure. Also your poker buddies were in an uproar. Will you please let them know you're okay?"

I tried Matt first. He was in court so I left a message.

It was Jorge's day off so I called him at home. After struggling through his excited torrent of Spanish, I deduced that the poker game broke up early. He and Hoa had been worried when I didn't show up, so they drove by the office and saw the cops still swarming around.

"We think at first it is you who is stabbed," he said. "Who is this animal who does this? Is he in jail?"

"I doubt it."

The police didn't have much to go on. I hadn't given them much of a description because it had been too dark…but it hadn't been dark when Harry had seen the man earlier yesterday. I remembered Harry handing me that flyer with his scribbled notes. What had he done with it after I handed it back?

I told Jorge I had to go.

"Okay, but you come for lunch, *si*? I am making something *muy especial*."

I promised I'd try. After I hung up, I unlocked my desk drawer, took out my gun, loaded it, and put it in my purse. I've never liked carrying around a cannon, but on the other hand I want something with stopping power. So I've settled on a .38 Smith and Wesson with a magnum load. Heavy but portable.

Today the weight felt reassuring as I hurried off downstairs. Harry's room was wide open, nobody around. Had the building management heard about him yet? Maybe they didn't read the papers.

The utility room was just a glorified broom closet, but surprisingly neat. In about ten minutes I'd searched the whole thing and found no sign of Harry's note. I did find a bottle of gin behind the Pine-sol, the seal unbroken.

I sat in Harry's rickety old chair and looked around. Of course, he may have thrown the note away, but, knowing Harry, I doubted it. I'd looked in his wallet the night before for an insurance card, so I knew the piece of paper wasn't there. Maybe he'd simply stuffed it in his pocket.

I got up and went in the lobby to peek outside. The unmarked car was still there. Brady must be tired of waiting for me to come in or call him. Well, there was no point of a visit to the police station until I went to see Harry and looked for the note, and to get to the hospital I needed my Mustang, which was sitting out in the parking lot with the only exit past the stakeout. I used the pay phone to dial the operator.

"Please—help—" I said. "Send the police. He's going to kill us—we're going to die—hurry—"

She tried to get me to dial 911, but I screamed hysterically about a bomb, gave her an address a block away, and quickly hung up. A minute later the beige sedan across the street took off.

I hotfooted it to my car and went the other way, heading for the hospital.

There was no problem with the staff this morning. Erik's money had worked wonders. They let me go in for a few minutes and sit beside Harry.

Against the white sheets of the narrow bed, Harry looked shrunken and gray. And small. Dwarfed by all the monitors and equipment. There were tubes in his arms, in his nose.

"Dammit, Harry," I said, tasting tears. "Maybe you'll learn to mind your own business."

I fumbled for a Kleenex and scrubbed my eyes. Blubbering wouldn't help either Mike or Harry. I looked around the cubicle. When Harry was checked in, his personal effects had been placed in a plastic bag. There was a skinny door in the wall by his bed. I opened it and discovered a closet—and the plastic bag.

The bloody T-shirt had been thrown away, but his cords were there, a few rusty stains spattering the front. I found the flyer carefully folded in a back pocket.

6 ft. 3 in. tl, 165 lb, blk hr, bwn eys, bshy brd, stud lf ear, blu jns, gry jkt, bts. TT rt arm, ratsnk.

Oh, Harry, if I ever wanted a new partner…

I squeezed his hand and left him, my mind racing, making plans. First stop was the police station. With Harry's description I just might be able to pick the guy out of a mug shot book. Of course I wanted the bastard in jail, but I also wanted some private conversation with him. Meanwhile, whoever hired him had to be pretty nervous. Maybe if I applied a little more pressure…

Out in the reception area, a big man leaned on the counter talking to the clerk, who gestured my way. Lieutenant Brady had gotten tired of leaving messages. He'd tracked me down.

THIRTEEN

"That was quite a stunt you pulled," Brady said.

"What was that?"

"Cute. You think I got nothing else to do but chase you all over town?"

"I was just on my way to your office. Shall we?"

He stayed on my heels to the parking lot and tailed me to the station. In his office, he shut the door, sat behind his desk, and eyed me sourly.

"You're a real pain in the ass," he said. "You and your half-baked ideas."

"And here I thought you'd come to the hospital out of concern for me and Harry."

"I'm sorry about Mr. Polk, but don't change the subject. The D.A. knows what you're doing. He knows your testimony against Morales is compromised. But we got lots of physical evidence, and believe me, that kid's going to do hard time. So, tell you what, Miss West. This is the end of your harassing people. I dug up the file on you." He tapped a folder. "That shooting out at the Thrifty Nifty Motel. I just might start digging into that. You've been getting some pretty good press lately, but you know how the newspapers love the juicy stuff. Bad for business. Maybe even put you *out* of business, you know?"

"Oh, I guess you haven't heard. I'm no longer self-employed."

I supplied the details and watched Erik's name work its magic.

"Well—" Brady said. "Well, uh, maybe I jumped the gun here. You're starting today, you say?"

"That's right."

I'd made the commitment and had every intention of honoring it. Of course, I still had a few hours left before I was officially on the Lundstrom payroll. Brady would hear that I was still asking questions and there'd be hell to pay. But for now, I had a little breathing room.

"Since I've got to wrap things up at my office, I'd really like to finish up with that report about the assault last night," I said.

"Right," he said, eager to cooperate.

Now that I'd used my new employment to distract Brady, I couldn't very well tell him my theory about my assailant. I just said Harry had seen the guy hanging around and had written down a description.

We fed the parameters into the Cal I.D. computer. Amazing how many bad guys had rattlesnakes tattooed on their arms. Twenty-six in all. My boy was number eleven. Edward Arnold Anson, aka Eddie Anson, aka Arnie Axton.

Brady wished me good luck on my new job and went to put out an A.P.B.

As I drove up to Anaheim Hills, I thought about two things—who had motive to kill Mr. Collins and who was nervous enough to send Eddie Anson calling.

Pamela had suddenly become an heiress. For that matter so had Carolyn, although the money was tied up for a few years. Was marriage to Pam in Warren's future plans? As for Ken, Pam's inheritance wouldn't be community property unless Ken could figure out a way to commingle it before the divorce. Was Ken that smart?

Or did money have nothing to do with it? Suppose Mr. Collins had spotted some kind of impropriety at Collins Electronics, and Warren was afraid he'd blow the whistle. Or suppose Joe and Lucy were lovers, and some other old geezer at the retirement home got jealous.

Suppose Charlie was right, and I ought to forget the whole damn thing.

That might have been a possibility before last night, but not now with Harry lying comatose in I.C.U. and the odds against his pulling through.

In Cresta Verde there was no company Mercedes in the Jacobses' driveway. The car count included the Jaguar, the Nissan Z, and a gold Cadillac, with the old Chevy still tucked away behind the garage.

Just as I left my car, Carolyn came out the front door, carrying an armload of books, fumbling in her purse for her keys.

"Carolyn?"

She looked up. Her face was raw and swollen. "Daddy's leaving," she said bleakly. "He's packing his things. They've been fighting all morning."

"Carolyn, I'm sorry."

I added all the conventional platitudes: Maybe it's for the best. Things will get better. Time heals. It didn't matter that they were all true and I really wanted to help.

She looked past me, obliquely studying the future, not believing a word of it. "I've got to go, Miss West. I don't want to be late for class."

After she got into the Nissan and drove off, I went up and rang the bell. Had I been the catalyst here? Who knows? Things had been bad before Pam's father died, so it was probably only a matter of time. Still…

The Asian woman answered the door, the same one who had hovered in the wings the first time I was here. I assumed she belonged to the old Chevy. She wore a dark dress with a white collar that approximated a maid's uniform. Thai, I thought, or Vietnamese. From someplace inside the house, voices rose and fell, reduced by distance to an angry hum.

"Busy now," she said. "You come back, pliss."

"I'm sorry. It's urgent." I stepped inside.

She stared at me for a second, then bobbed her head and scurried off.

In a few minutes, Pamela came into the entry, the maid trailing behind. Pam wore tailored navy slacks, a matching navy cardigan over a cream silk blouse. Her pale skin was flushed, her eyes the color of flint.

"I told Nguyet that we didn't want to see anybody," Pam said coldly. "Apparently she didn't get the message across."

"Don't blame her. I pushed my way in."

"All right, you're in. Do I have to call the police to get you out?"

"That's pretty drastic, isn't it? You know how the police operate. They'll send squad cars with flashing lights, maybe sirens, and the whole neighborhood will be out gawking. All I want is to talk to you and Ken for a few minutes, but if you'd rather deal with the cops—"

She waved the maid away and said curtly, "Ken's in the shop. This way."

I followed her to a door at the end of the hall that opened into the garage. Now I understood why the cars were always parked on the driveway. The garage had been outfitted with a workbench, a table saw, shelves of supplies. Several large pieces of antique furniture stood around in various stages of restoration. The place smelled of varnish and oil and wood dust. I realized the antiques throughout the house and the desk at the jewelry shop must be Ken's handiwork.

Ken stood at the workbench packing flat metal cans of paint remover and lacquer thinner into a box marked Solvents. His faded Levi's sagged and the shadows under his eyes were tinged with plum.

"Delilah." There was no surprise in his voice, only resignation. He picked up a rag from the bench and began wiping his hands.

"All right," Pam said to me. "You're here."

"Okay," I said. "First of all, let's get one thing straight. The only reason I've been asking questions is that I have some real doubts about what happened to your father."

"My father was run down by that Morales boy and left in the street to die."

"That's partially true. Mike did run over Mr. Collins, and then he panicked and took off. But it's very likely your father was already dead when Mike got there."

"You're sick, you know that? You think one of us killed him? Who? Me? Carolyn? We get all the money." She turned on Ken, who still scrubbed at his hands with the cleaning rag. "Are you going to just stand there?"

"What do you want me to do?"

"Make her stop it."

"Pam, I really don't see how."

"Oh, yes, make excuses. You're good at that. It's about the only thing you are good at."

It sounded like an old argument, one I didn't want to hear. "Ken isn't going to keep me from going ahead with this investigation. Neither is Warren. Because your father's death isn't the only thing I'm investigating now."

"What do you mean?" Ken stood very still and stared at me. At least he'd stopped wiping his hands.

"Somebody sent this creep to see me last night. He was supposed to scare me off, but a friend of mine got in the way. He's an old man too, Pam, like your father. And now he's in the hospital."

"And I suppose you think we had something to do with that too," Pam said. "Now I *know* you're crazy. You have five minutes, Miss West. If you're not gone by then I really will call the police."

She went out and slammed the door.

"She means it," Ken said. "You can't talk to her once she's made up her mind." He tossed the oily rag into the box of solvents and began sorting aimlessly through the tools on the bench. "Your friend—is he going to be all right?"

"I wish I knew."

"What you said to Pam—you really think this attack is connected to Joe?"

"Yes. And as soon as the police pick the guy up, he'll confirm it."

"You got a good look at him? Enough to give them a description?"

"Better than that," I said. "We've already got a make on him. We know his name."

"That's great then. It'll be over soon—if he talks."

"They always do. Offer them a deal, they sing their little hearts out." I gestured to his things. "Where are you going from here?"

"A hotel, I guess. I can store some of this stuff at the shop. The rest…I'll have to think of something." He picked up another rag and went back to wiping his hands. "Delilah? Maybe you're wrong about what happened last night. Sometimes things aren't always the way they seem."

I glanced at my watch. "My time's up. Can I go out through the garage door?"

"Sure." He pushed a button mounted on the wall and the big door slid open.

"Tell Pam what I said, will you? And Carolyn."

"Carolyn?" He looked sick. "My God—you really do suspect— she and Pam—no, God no."

"I hope you're right," I said, and I did.

But I found myself remembering the blood orange Charlie had eaten for breakfast. Perfectly ordinary on the outside, but when he cut into it…

"I am right," Ken said. "Carolyn would never've hurt Joe. Neither would Pam."

But what about you, Ken? I wondered as the garage door rumbled down. What about you?

FOURTEEN

Leaving Cresta Verde, I debated. It was close to lunchtime. I needed to make some phone calls, but I could do that from the Sanchezes' as well as my office. Besides, I was hungry.

While Jorge put the finishing touches on lunch, I checked in with Rita. Nothing urgent. No call from the hospital so I called them. Harry was the same. I kept going down my list. Matt was out. I left word that I would be at the jail visiting Mike at two. Could he meet me?

Next I called Lucy Taylor. Since I'd had no luck getting in touch with Greenspace, I intended to ask for the names of the people who usually attended meetings. It would be slow going, but I'd just have to question all of them. I hadn't forgotten that standard motive for murder I'd put in third place—passion.

"My dear, are you all right?" Lucy asked. "I saw in the paper about that awful man who tried to mug you."

I assured her I was. If she'd read that article and made the connection, that meant she must know who I was.

She admitted she did. "I wormed it out of poor Ken. I wish you'd told me right away. Just the thought of somebody deliberately killing Joe—and now this awful thing last night...I'm so terrified sometimes with all these muggings and killings going on. Did you get a look at the man?"

"Good enough, and it wasn't just a mugging, Lucy."

"Oh, my dear, what else could it be?"

"Somebody trying to throw a scare in me."

"Well, I guess it didn't work, did it? You're certainly a brave young woman, Delilah. I just wish there was something I could do to help you—"

"There is." I told her what I wanted.

"Well, of course. I'll make up a list. But you know, Delilah, I have an idea. Why don't I talk to some of these people? Maybe I could save you some time."

"That's nice of you, Lucy, but—"

"No, I meant what I said. I want to do what I can. I could ask them if they were at the meeting, if they saw Joe there. Wouldn't that help?"

"Well, sure." It might speed up checking on when and how Joe left the meeting. I could dig for the gossip later.

"It's settled then. If I find out anything, where can I reach you? At your office? Maybe I should have your home phone."

"I'll be in and out. It's best for me if you leave word with my answering service."

I thanked her and rang off, then dialed Collins Electronics, catching Bill Irwin before he went to lunch.

"If you're trying to reach Warren, I don't think he'll talk to you," Bill said.

"That's what I figured, so I thought maybe you'd pass along a message."

"What?" he asked warily.

"Somebody sent me a warning last night. The deliveryman was very tall and nasty, and he carried a knife. Tell Warren I identified the man, and the police will have him soon."

"Uh-huh," he said. "I take it there's a reason for this message."

"Why, Bill, and you said you're a private eye buff. Just tell him, okay?"

So…pressure points covered. Now what? I was running out of calls except the one that always got me nowhere.

"Let's eat," Jorge sang out, or the Spanish to that effect.

I could smell simmering meat and chili and tomatillos. "*Un momento,*" I yelled back, and dialed the Greenspace number. What the heck?

Two rings and a woman's voice said, "Thank you for calling Greenspace. We can't speak to you right now—"

Strike three. I hung up and went to join Jorge.

I told him about my new job, and we toasted my good fortune with a Corona. Only one beer for me since I was driving. "So I guess I'll have my own shower again," I said. "You won't have to put up with me popping in."

"A friend is never a bother," he said. "Be sure you do not forget us when you're living in this big house."

No possibility of that, I told him with a lump in my throat.

I asked him to remember me to Consuelo and the children and the poker gang and left for the Orange County Jail. During the drive I thought about Greenspace and what I thought was, it was damned peculiar, a charity closing its office for days at a stretch. What if somebody with lots of money called? Of course, now Mr. (or Mrs.) Big Bucks could leave a message because…

Because somebody had turned on the answering machine.

I sat at a stop sign, thinking about that until the car behind me honked indignantly. I had my left-turn signal on but turned right instead. That got me another horn blast as I pulled into an Arco station and parked in front of a phone booth.

Of course, Miss Ferguson could've used a remote controller to turn on the machine. Still…The chained metal cover the phone book belonged in was empty. Rather than hassle with Information, I called Rita and had her look up Greenspace for me and give me the address.

I'd have to detour, but not by far. Matt had said the organization was low profile. The office space on the edge of the Santa Ana barrio definitely fit that definition. It looked as though the guy who did my building had been working here.

Two floors, small cubicles. Greenspace was downstairs on the corner. A minimum of parking in back. I pulled in. The lot was full. I was on my way out again when I saw a young woman come out the back door of the Greenspace office. I stopped and turned to look. She inserted a key in the door, locking it.

I left the Mustang double parked and hurried over.

"Excuse me—Miss Ferguson?"

"No, I'm sorry. Amy's not here." She had long, straight sun-streaked hair and huge round glasses. She balanced a big stack of brochures and outgoing mail.

"When will she be back? I've been trying to reach her for days."

"Oh, well, that was my fault. Amy was up in Santa Barbara and I was off and I forgot to turn on the machine." She shifted her load of brochures, holding them with her chin.

"Could I give you a hand with those?" I asked.

"Yes—sure. Thanks."

I took part of the stack and trailed her to a little red Hyundai, glancing at the envelopes. Most of them were office mail with the Greenspace logo, but one had a little printed computer label that read: Tess Anderson.

"Things always pile up when you're away, don't they?" I said. "You need a vacation to recover from your vacation. Tess—it's Tess, isn't it? When will Miss Ferguson be back?"

"Oh, she's here. You just missed her." Tess put the brochures on top of her car and took a key ring from her purse that must have weighed as much as my gun. She never questioned how I knew her name.

"Just my luck," I said ruefully. "Funny, though, when I called earlier, the machine was on."

"Are you the one who hung up? Amy was so busy with the dinner tonight and all, she decided to screen the calls. I can give her a message if you like." Tess unlocked the hatch and began loading her things.

"It's really urgent." I handed her the stack of brochures. "Is she at home? Could you give me that number?"

"Oh, no, I couldn't do that. Anyway, I think she went straight down to the Yacht Club."

"The Yacht Club! The dinner!" I did everything but smack my forehead. "Oh, my God, it *is* tonight, isn't it?"

"Yes—"

"I knew it. I had this feeling, you know? My assignment editor had it down for tomorrow and I kept telling him—boy, am I lucky I bumped into you. And Miss Ferguson will be so pleased. I'm from the *Daily Press* and I'm supposed to be covering the dinner. Jeez, just wait till my editor hears how he screwed up. Listen, you know, now I'm wondering if he got the rest of the details straight. Would you mind just giving them to me again? Just in case?"

Balboa Bay Yacht Club. Cocktails at seven; dinner at eight; black tie. Two hundred dollars a pop.

I was sure I had a press card somewhere.

I secured my gun in the glove compartment before I went into the jail to meet Matt. He waited in the reception area, pacing, eyeing his watch.

"Sorry I'm late."

"I have to be back in my office in half an hour." He gestured for the guard, who unlocked a door and led us through.

"Hell of a note what happened last night," Matt said as we walked. "I tried to call you all day. You okay?"

I said I was and gave him a report on Harry.

The guard escorted us into a visiting room. "Do we need to talk before we see Mike?" Matt asked me.

I shook my head and he told the guard to bring Mike in. When the man left, Matt turned to me. "You want to give me a hint? I figure you've come to say good-bye."

"You figure wrong."

"You turned down the job?"

"Not exactly—"

The guard brought Mike in. He looked thinner and he hadn't shaved. The stubble didn't do much for his zits and oily skin. I pictured him in front of a jury. They'd all be hiding their money and wondering where he kept his switchblade.

He slouched into a chair and stared at me coldly. "So, how about it? You got something that's gonna get me outta here?"

"Not yet, but I've talked to a lot of people, and I've come up with a few leads and—"

"Right. *Right.* You got nothing, don't you? *Nada.* Zilch. Zip. Don't shit me about this, Miss West. I want it straight."

I felt like belting him across the mouth, but I held my temper. "Okay, straight. No, I don't have anything solid yet but there's a good chance I will soon."

I told him about the assault on me, about Harry's being stabbed, about my theory.

"Do the police know about this?" Matt asked.

"A waste of time," I said. "Take my word. What I'm hoping is they'll pick this guy up pretty quick. Then I'm going straight to Tom Devaney with my story."

Mike was a quick study. "You think Devaney'll make Anson an offer, get him to cop a plea?"

"I think it's our best shot."

"A pretty damn long one, if you ask me," Matt said. "The guy could be long gone by now. They might never catch him."

"I said it's our best shot, not the only one. I'm finally going to get to talk to the woman from Greenspace." I explained that Amy Ferguson was back in town, and I planned to see her later. Then I turned to Mike. "There's something else I have to tell you."

Matt got a here-it-comes look on his face.

"I can't work on this full time anymore," I said. "This is straight, Mike, okay? I'm flat broke. I'm living in my office and bumming showers and meals off my friends. I've been offered a good job, and

I'm going to take it. That doesn't mean I'll stop working on your case. It'll just take a little longer, that's all."

Mike looked at me, any hostility tempered by the amazing discovery that I was human just like him. "Okay, sure. I mean, you gotta eat. Have you told my mom yet?"

"No, but I will soon."

"I'll do it," Mike said. "She might get all weirded out thinking how I'll take it, but if she sees I'm cool—yeah, that'll be better."

"Okay." I stood up and Matt went to signal the guard. "You hang tough. Maybe we'll get a break soon."

"Yeah, sure." A cynical smile. Life had never given Mike Morales a break. Why start now?

The guard waited for him at the door. On the threshold, Mike paused. "Delilah?" A hesitation while he tried to decide what to say that wasn't too mushy. Finally he said, "Watch your back."

"Mike's right," Matt said as we retraced our steps to the reception area. "You ever think that this—what's his name? Anson? You ever think he might pay you a return visit?"

"I've thought about it."

"Probably a good idea if you stayed someplace else besides your office. Look—" He took out a card and wrote something on it, gave it to me. "My home address and phone number. You're welcome if you don't mind sleeping on my couch. I'll even promise—no more holier-than-thou remarks."

I thanked him but told him I already had a place to go.

He held open the front door, and we went outside. The clouds had broken, and the sun poured through, a bright honey-gold, deliciously warm. But it didn't last. By the time I got to my car, a thunderhead boiled up in the west and it was dark again. The wind had a raw, chill edge.

I shivered and remembered to take my gun from the glove compartment and put it back in my purse.

FIFTEEN

I had some time before the Greenspace dinner, so I went back to the office to pack. An ugly purple twilight had arrived early, shadowing the parking lot. I unzipped my purse, keeping the gun handy, and moved warily as I left my car.

I got an adrenaline high from slipping cautiously up the stairs and entering my dark office, but nothing else happened. I expelled a shaky breath. Better watch it, or I'd be blasting typewriters and filing cabinets. I locked the door behind me and put on the kettle for coffee.

Most of my things were in storage. All I needed to move tonight were the clothes, toiletries, and a minimum of personal stuff that I kept at the office. The black silk would have to do for the Yacht Club. I kept out the dress and a black wool shawl and folded the rest into my big suitcase.

The rent was paid here for another two weeks. I'd have to give notice, call the phone company, do something with the furniture.

The back of my throat hurt, and I swallowed hard. Don't start, I told myself. So—big deal.

A dinky office in a rundown neighborhood. I'd been here only three years. Leaving the place I shared with Jack had been a wrenching experience. At the time, I had thought it was the most difficult thing I'd ever have to do. Now I know better. Offices are easy. Letting go of dreams, *that's* the hard part.

"A fresh start, Delilah. Orange County. Upscale crime and all that sunshine. West and West Detective Agency. What do you think?"

"West and West? What's this? Another proposal?"

"*Yep. Package deal. Ah, come on, darlin'. Make an honest man of me.*"

So here I am, Jack. Now what do I do?

A moot question since my suitcase was already packed.

The kettle whistled. I mixed up some coffee and ate the last granola bar, remembering the dinner at Erik's and wondering if the staff ate that well. At least they ate, although there was probably a kitchen in the apartment and I'd be expected to fend for myself.

I called the hospital for an update on Harry—no change—then checked in with Rita. I hadn't said a word to her about the job offer, and I didn't want to tell her over the phone.

"Are you busy later?" I asked. "I thought I'd stop by."

"Sure. We've got aerobics, but we'll be home by nine." She reported a dramatic decrease in messages and wondered if that was good news or bad.

"Good, I hope." At least Brady hadn't called to chew me out. On the other hand he hadn't called to say they'd arrested Eddie Anson.

After I finished my coffee, I went to the ladies' room to brush my teeth and wash my face. Came back and got dressed. When I was ready to go, I dug around and found the press card—expired, but some judicious forgery extended it for another six months.

My suitcase was ready, but I could come back for it later. No need to wrestle with it in my good clothes and heels.

Outside the pavement was still dry although the sky looked heavy and leaden. I plodded through rush-hour traffic and arrived at the Balboa Bay Yacht Club at six-thirty. My gun was back in the glove compartment—a real drag juggling the damn thing, which was one reason why I rarely carried it.

I flashed the press card at the gate and talked my way in. In front of the club, I got out and gave my keys to a valet, snuggling into my shawl as I hurried inside. No problem getting past the guard at the parking lot entrance, but the fellow on the door had eagle eyes, experienced at spotting gate-crashers.

"Even if you are press, you still need an invitation," he said, pleasant but implacable.

"Oh, *Lord*." I feigned panic and pawed through my purse. "I *know* my editor gave me one. Where *is* it?"

I was getting ready to throw myself on his mercy, pleading unemployment and disgrace, but I was spared laying on the histrionics by a familiar figure getting out of a red Hyundai, juggling an armload of boxes.

"Tess, hello," I called as she came in the door. "Looks like you've got your hands full again. Let me help."

The doorman got ready to voice his objections so I hurried on. "Listen, somehow I misplaced my invitation so if you could just vouch for me—"

She did, and I followed her in, ignoring his sour look.

I'd been in the Yacht Club before and thought what I always did, that it was much smaller and much plainer than the name implied. Only the view lived up to expectations. At night the harbor was inky glass with endless rows of sleek ships riding quietly. The cost of mooring fees alone was enough to keep a third-world country afloat.

Near the permanent bar, a horseshoe buffet table was being set up. A tall red-haired woman in a white beaded dress conferred with one of the chefs. When she saw us, she broke off and hurried over. Slim, with flawless skin and big green eyes. She wore huge silver filigree earrings that caught the light.

"Tess, I was beginning to worry."

"The traffic was the pits," Tess said, dumping her boxes of brochures and name tags on a table. As I followed suit, she added, "Oh, Amy, this is—sorry, did you tell me your name?"

Amy stared at me expectantly.

"Delilah West."

"Of the *Daily Press*," Tess added. "She came by today and just missed you."

"I see." Either the *Press* really did have a Delilah West on the payroll or Amy Ferguson recognized my name. "Tess, can you start setting up by yourself? I'm sure Miss West will need some background material. Miss West?"

She led the way to a table in a back corner, past the buffet decorated with ice sculptures of palm trees and exotic birds, crowded with huge platters of sushi and sashimi, lobster, shrimp and crab claws, *carnitas,* mounds of caviar. The tables were set with real linen cloths and napkins, heavy sterling. Crystal glasses waited to be filled with Dom Pérignon.

Amy, the perfect hostess, summoned a waiter and offered me a drink. I asked for Perrier, and she told him to make it two.

After he left, I said, "I get the feeling I can drop the Lois Lane act."

"It would save time. I know about Mr. Collins's death, of course, and I heard you were—" She sought a word, settled for "—involved. I'm not sure why you want to talk to me."

"I need to know if Mr. Collins came to the meeting that night before he died."

"Yes, he rarely missed one."

"He was very involved in your organization then?"

She nodded, accepting mineral water from the waiter, sipping it. "What do you know about Greenspace, Miss West?"

"Not much."

"Well—" She glanced at her watch. "Pollution is our blanket concern, of course. But air pollution has had plenty of press, and the public is very much aware of it. Our main thrust is toxic waste, the chemicals that get dumped in the ground and pollute the soil and the water table. Joe was very active with our group, maybe because he was in business most of his life. He really knew where the bodies were buried—or rather the chemical garbage. He was a wonderful man. We'll miss him."

"After the meeting was over, did you see him leave?"

"I'm afraid not. I usually get stuck for a while answering questions. No, I didn't notice him go."

"Did he speak to you that evening?"

"Well, he said hello, but I think that's about all."

"He didn't mention where he was going afterward or if he was meeting somebody?"

She shook her head.

"What about when you left the clubhouse? Did you see him then or notice anything unusual? Anybody hanging around?"

"No, nothing. I wish I could help you, but—" She glanced at her watch again and stood up. "I am sorry, but I have to be at the door when people arrive. You understand? But I would like to help you if I can. I'll tell you what. I'll think about the meeting tonight and see if I can remember anything else."

While she talked she maneuvered me swiftly toward the door, beckoning the doorman and adding, "Call me, okay?"

I said I would, appreciating the finesse but recognizing a hustle when I saw one.

The valet brought my Mustang. It looked every bit the work-horse among the Jags and Maseratis and Bentleys. At the exit to Coast Highway, I saw a white Rolls entering the lot and got a glimpse of the driver.

A sickening lurch in my stomach—dread, recognition, resignation. I drove a few hundred feet away and turned into the nearest restaurant parking lot. Somebody was pulling out of an end space. A Cadillac waited for the slot. I nosed out the Caddy, bolted from my car, and walked rapidly back to the Yacht Club.

A crush of autos now, people pouring in, so it was easy to slip past the guard and head through the parking lot. I pleaded a lost wallet to the doorman, brushing past before he could stop me.

Inside there was a swirl of glittering gowns, plenty of white tuxes—the beautiful people come to party—but I had no trouble recognizing Erik Lundstrom. He was standing next to Amy, his arm around her waist, her face tilted up toward his.

Amy, the hostess. Oh, yes indeed.

Such an elegant match, the two of them. Like me, Amy was almost young enough to be his daughter, but there was nothing familial in the way she looked at him or the way he leaned down to brush her lips with his.

SIXTEEN

Back at the office, my suitcase waited, packed and ready. A bad joke. I unzipped it, pulled out jeans and a sweater, and changed my clothes.

I couldn't stay there, so I went out again and drove around aimlessly. That was the problem with my life, I decided. I had no place to go.

This was not something I wanted to discuss with my friends. Anyway, I was too mad to be articulate and, yes, dammit, jealous. There was disappointment too, a big sour lump in my throat. And a growing feeling of being manipulated, set up, used.

Connect the dots: Erik and Amy; Erik and Charlie; Amy and Joseph Collins. I didn't have a complete picture yet, just a shadowy outline, but I knew it would be very ugly.

I stopped for a traffic light and realized I was a block away from the hospital. From the hospital lobby I called Rita's service and left word for her that something had come up so I wouldn't be stopping by.

Up in I.C.U., I discovered that Harry's condition had been changed from critical to serious and he'd been moved to a private room. I went and sat by him. The nurse explained he was slowly coming out of the coma, that really now it was more like a deep sleep.

He looked better, his skin tone a little pinker, and he was breathing on his own, so the oxygen tube had been removed. One thing Erik's money had done was to buy Harry the best care. Only maybe the *reason* everything was covered wasn't because Erik was generous. Maybe he had a guilty conscience.

I remembered Matt saying that there was a lot of money behind Greenspace. Erik's money? Greenspace was definitely the pivotal point. Joe Collins died just after he attended that meeting in Linda Vista Park. And Amy—Amy left town.

And let's not forget good old helpful, concerned Charlie. Calling me up as soon as he read about the hit and run in the paper, checking on me. Then—what a coincidence—he just happened to know about this terrific job. Maybe there was an opening on Erik's security staff. If not, well, easy enough to create one. Easy for Erik to turn on the charm…

Visiting hours were long since over and I was sick of guessing games. I kissed Harry's cheek, left the hospital, and headed for the coast.

The guard at the Lundstrom estate's entrance gate recognized me and checked my name off a list. "Do you know where your quarters are, Miss West? Why don't I buzz Vincent and have him give you a hand?"

"That's okay. I can manage."

Something in my tone alerted him, I suppose. Or maybe it was the way I looked. He probably had regular seminars on clenched jawlines and narrowed eyes. Vincent was waiting for me when I pulled into the huge circular driveway and parked next to the Rolls. He opened my door.

"Hi, how's it going?" His coat was unbuttoned, his hands casually ready to reach for the gun I'd bet was tucked in his belt at the small of his back.

My .38 was still in the glove compartment. Wasn't it always? I didn't think Vincent would be too happy if I took it out.

"Just great," I said. "The boss inside?"

"It's a little late for business. Why don't we get you settled and you can talk to him in the morning."

The sensible thing to do was to cool it, wait, plan some strategy. Oh, yeah, I knew that. A mule with blinders, Jack used to say. Jack knew me, all right.

"This won't take long," I said.

I headed for the entrance, but Vince was quicker, closing the distance and moving in front to bar the way.

"Erik told me to check in with him, Vince. So if you've got a problem, I think you'd better talk to him."

He hesitated, debating, probably wondering if the gateman was getting a little paranoid. Then he stepped aside and let me go in, but he stayed close behind, saying "He's in the study."

Study? I hazarded a guess and went for the room I'd sat in that first night I visited here, having a quiet drink with Erik and Charlie.

Bingo.

Erik was there and—surprise, surprise—so was Amy Ferguson, sharing one of the three sofas, having a brandy, looking into Erik's baby blues. They'd changed into casual clothes, Erik in his faded jeans and an L.L. Bean sweater, Amy wearing wool slacks and a taupe silk blouse, long sleeved with the cuffs rolled up.

"Erik, hi!" I said. "And, Amy, how nice."

Vincent was right on my heels. "She insisted on seeing you, Mr. Lundstrom."

"That's all right, Vincent. Delilah, come on in." Erik stood up. The perfect gentleman.

Amy looked flustered. "Erik, I had no idea she connected me to you."

"Oh, don't worry," I said. "You did just fine, Amy. It was the timing that was off. Erik driving in just as I was driving out—"

"Delilah, before you start jumping to conclusions, sit down and let's talk," Erik said.

"What should we talk about? The way you and Charlie went to such great lengths to stop me from finding out how Joe Collins died?"

"*How* he died," Amy said.

"You do know, don't you? You were there."

"My God." Amy gasped. "Erik—"

"Was it an accident? Did he wander in front of your car? Or did he have a big lech for you? Maybe he came on a little too strong and—"

"Okay, that's it." Erik clamped hard fingers around my arm.

Suddenly my anger evaporated as I remembered the acres of wild coastal hills outside, the deep ravines like the one I'd seen behind the house.

"I told somebody I was coming here," I said. "Matthew Scott, the public defender for the Morales boy. If I don't call him back, he'll phone the police."

"Don't be an idiot." Erik hustled me out the door. Vincent stood just outside, instantly alert. Erik told him, "See that Miss Ferguson gets home."

Did Erik really think I'd go quietly? Was he planning to handcuff me, tie me up? In the front hall, he let go of my arm and put on an old leather jacket, then held open the front door.

"I'd suggest you follow me in your own car, but I'm afraid you might get some dumb idea about heading for the nearest sheriff's station," he said as we left the house. "I'm certainly not going to compromise everything at this point."

"Compromise what?"

"If you'd stop reacting and use your head—" He opened the door on the passenger's side of the Lamborghini and waited for me to climb in.

I could say that my brilliant deductive powers kicked in and I put it all together, but the truth is I just didn't believe that Erik Lundstrom was planning to take me out someplace and put a bullet through my head.

I got in.

We shot off into the darkness.

"You going to tell me where we're going?"

"You'll see," he said curtly.

After that he got busy handling the driving as we hurtled along on the rain-slick pavement, weaving in and out of traffic. I tightened my seat belt and kept my eyes off the speedometer. A little like doing your algebra homework while riding on Thunder Mountain at Disneyland, but I did put two and two together.

When we exited the freeway and headed for Collins Electronics, I was glad I could still come up with an occasional right answer.

Erik slowed down to cruise past the front entrance of the plant. The gate was locked, the guard house empty. A few spotlights illuminated the buildings, but it all had a deserted look. No vehicles in the lot; none on the street.

Collins Electronics took up a whole block. Erik went down to the corner, made a right, followed the chain-linked perimeter of the parking lot. Turned right again.

Another industrial plant was on the opposite side of the street, the two companies back to back. There were several detached semi-trailers sitting around in the other company's back lot and hugging the shadow of one of them was a van with a perfect view of Collins's loading dock.

We went past quickly so I got only a glimpse of the activity over there. Some lights, a truck backed up to the dock, men moving around.

Erik kept going, circled the block, and parked out of sight on the cross street. He picked up a cellular phone, dialed, waited, then said, "It's Erik. We're around the corner, be there in a minute." Pause. "Yes, I said *we*. Who do you think?"

He broke the connection and we got out and walked back, staying in the shadows, working our way toward the van. From the Collins loading dock on the other side of the street came metallic clanks and thumps, the rumble of a forklift. When we reached the trailer that provided cover for the van, Erik touched my arm and we stopped to take a closer look.

Several men were moving barrels into a semi. There were no markings on either the metal containers or the truck. "What's inside?" I asked in a whisper.

"Cleaners. Acids. Trichloroethane, acetone."

We slipped around the trailer and Erik tapped softly on the van's door. The door slid open. The interior was lighted only by the glow of an elaborate set of instruments. Still, it was bright enough for me to recognize the two men operating the surveillance gear. Charlie I had expected. The second man who sat at a console was Bill Irwin. He flipped me a little salute.

As soon as the door slid into place, Charlie switched on a dim overhead light. "I guess you were right," he said to Erik. "She figured it out."

"Not soon enough." I looked around. Remote video. High-gain directional bugging equipment. "You always did have the best stuff, Charlie. So this is the big secret?"

"Yes," Erik said. "*All* of it. Joe got wind of the midnight dumping and went to Amy with his suspicions. I brought Charlie in to investigate." He turned to Charlie. "Will we have enough?"

"This and the documentation Bill got on the inside—more than enough, I'd say."

"You couldn't just explain to me what you were doing?" I asked.

"How many times did I see you screw up lately?" Charlie asked. "I understand how you were using Joe's accident for a little free publicity. That's okay. Hell, in your place, I might do the same myself. But you think I'm gonna blab about a confidential operation? This was strictly need-to-know."

My friend. My pal. If everything hadn't been bolted down, I'd have smashed him over the head with a piece of his high-tech equipment.

"You bastard," I said. "While you were busy sabotaging my investigation, another old man almost got killed."

"You mean Mr. Polk?" Erik asked.

I nodded.

"Charlie, you assured me that the attack on Mr. Polk had nothing to do with Joe's death."

"She's just guessing," Charlie said.

"Still, if there's any possibility—" Erik turned to me. "What can I do to help?"

"Answer a question. Did Mr. Collins ever mention he thought Warren Kurtz was suspicious? Maybe Mr. Collins let something slip about Charlie's surveillance?"

"He never said anything to me. Charlie?"

"Nope."

"Something you should know," Bill said, keeping his attention on the console. "Warren was here the night that Mr. Collins died. I was tailing him. I think he was waiting for the disposal crew to come, but they never showed."

"So he didn't do the job personally." I had a good candidate for the hit man.

"Doesn't wash," Charlie said shortly. "Allowing you could be right about this—which I'm not—I could see Kurtz getting into an argument with Collins, maybe a little pushing and shoving. But to buy a hit...over this?"

"Charlie's right." Bill looked up from the video monitor. "Greenspace is going to generate a lot of bad press when Collins Electronics gets charged with dumping chemical waste. Enough so the government will have to get into it, but what are we talking about? Some stiff fines. A slap on the wrist. Warren might lose his job. You think that's enough of a motive to kill Joe?"

"Not by itself. But he's involved with Pam Jacobs. Her father's death makes her a rich woman."

"Sounds to me like the daughter should be number one on your list," Charlie put in.

"Charlie," Bill said. "They're moving."

"Right." Charlie turned to us. "We have to roll. I'll call you later, Erik."

We got out and worked our way back to the Lamborghini. Erik headed for the freeway. Driving south, he stayed with the traffic, a smooth safe ride. The tires hissed on the wet pavement, and the windshield wipers moved rhythmically.

Less than twenty-four hours ago I'd sat in the backseat of the Rolls, drifting off to sleep in Erik's arms.

"You've got a right to be angry," he said finally. "But I want you to know I believed Joe was the victim of a hit and run. We'd put a lot into this investigation—Joe put a lot into it. I didn't want to see it go down the drain. And Charlie convinced me that could happen if you kept poking around in Joe's death. He said you never give up."

"He got that right."

Erik exited the freeway, stopped at the signal, and turned to look at me. "I did have an opening on my staff, Delilah, so the job offer seemed a perfect way to distract you. Then Charlie brought you over…" He smiled. The light turned green but he sat for a couple of seconds before driving off. "Charlie's usually a good judge of character, but this time—well, you were not as advertised. Not at all."

We glided toward the coast. The high-rise office buildings at Newport's Fashion Island floated in the mist. I felt drained and tired.

"I want you to know one thing," Erik went on. "Last night—that had nothing to do with—" He hesitated.

"With the lying, deceitful scheme you and Charlie cooked up," I supplied.

"Ouch." He shot me a rueful grin." I came to the hospital as a friend."

"If you say so."

He was the friendly type. Me. Amy. Jealous again. I admit it.

"Charlie told me something else about you, Delilah. I was hoping he was wrong. He said you take things hard and you never forget."

"He was right again."

Erik was silent as we arrowed up the dark road, past the guard gate, to his house. That was fine with me. I had nothing else to say.

He parked on the circular drive and then, while I fumbled for the door handle, he added, "Delilah, if you need any help finding Joe's murderer, call Charlie. I'll tell him to do whatever you ask and put it on my bill."

"Nice of you."

I fumbled some more but could not get the damn door open. He reached across me to grab the handle, his arm pressing against my breasts, his face close. Too dark to see those blue, blue eyes of his clearly. Good thing.

"I wish this had turned out differently," he said softly. "I wanted you here, Delilah. I still do."

Along with Amy, I had to assume.

He pulled the latch, opening the door, and moved away. I'd been wrong to think I had nothing else to say. There was one thing.

"Good-bye, Erik," I said.

SEVENTEEN

There was no place to go but my office. I pulled into the parking lot behind the building and shut off the engine. Water puddled on the patchy old asphalt. Dim lighting and the wet sheen showed up all the stains on the pavement. Had it rained enough to wash away Harry's blood?

I sat there until my feet got cold, then started the engine and drove away. I had no idea where I was going. I just knew I couldn't spend the night on my office floor.

A motel? Not with the one dollar I had left in my pocket. My credit cards had hit their limits months ago. I could always go to Rita's. Or Jorge and Consuelo's. But then I'd have to deal with their friendly pity and concerned prying.

There was another option.

Waiting for a stop light, I rummaged in my purse and came up with Matthew Scott's card, the one with his home address scribbled on the back.

Matt's condo complex was set up like a college exam in logic. I finally left my car and set out on foot. And then, of course, it started to pour. By the time I found the right unit, my hair was plastered to my head. Did I really need to be found on Matt's doorstep, a poor little waif in from the storm?

As I hesitated, a dog began barking inside the condo, a fierce deep-throated alarm. I heard Matt say, "Okay, all right. That's enough now." Before I could bolt, the outside light went on, and the door opened.

"Delilah?" He wore a green flannel shirt, old chinos with a frayed hole near the riveted edge of the right pocket, worn Top-Siders with no socks.

"You said if I needed a place to stay—is the offer still open?"

"Of course, come on in." To the dog, "Ozzie, knock it off."

His territory properly defended, Ozzie was all tail-wagging friendliness, jumping around, a small tan and white dust mop dog with soulful eyes and an underbite that reminded me of an old Buick.

"I can lock him in the kitchen," Matt said.

"No, don't do that."

I bent to pat the fuzzy head, dripping water on Matt's three square feet of tiled entry.

"Delilah, you're soaked." Matt took my coat. "I've got a fire going. Go and sit while I find you some dry clothes."

The living room was comfortable and lived-in, done in grays and blues, remarkably neat except for open law books, file folders, and legal pads strewn on the coffee table and couch. In the fireplace, gas logs blazed, unscreened. I sat on the brick hearth, close to the flames. I was shivering now, my teeth chattering.

Matt came back with a sweatsuit, took one look at me, said, "Jesus," and hustled me into the bathroom. He turned on the shower, steaming hot. "Can you manage?"

I nodded.

"You're sure? Okay, but sing out if you need me."

After he left, I stripped off my clothes and got under the blissful warmth, stayed there until I stopped shaking. Then I toweled myself dry and got dressed. The shoulders of the sweatshirt drooped to my elbows, so I rolled up the sleeves. The pants had a drawstring waist, baggy but warm.

I came out of the bathroom to find Ozzie waiting by the door. He barked and led the way to the kitchen, which was filled with a hot, tomatoey odor. Matt poured soup from a pot into a bowl.

"Smells great," I said.

"Home grown." He pointed to a Campbell's can. "Go on back by the fire. I'll bring this in."

The tray he brought also contained buttered sourdough bread, a bottle of Cabernet Sauvignon, and two glasses. He shoved aside some books, making room on the coffee table for the tray, and poured the wine while I hungrily spooned the soup into my mouth.

He waited, sipping, while I polished off the soup and mopped the bowl with a bread crust.

"Do you want to talk about it?" he asked.

"Do I have to?" I shared the bread crust with the dog.

"No."

"Thanks."

He refilled the glasses, then took the tray to the kitchen. I sat on the floor, leaning against the couch and facing the fire. In a minute he came back, dropped down beside me, his shoulder touching mine. The dog jumped up on the sofa, lay with his chin on his paws, sighed. The flames crackled and hissed.

For a moment I remembered sitting beside Erik that first night in his study, but the image came and went. I'd stumbled into a remarkable place, isolated, suspended in time, where it was possible to put the world on hold for a while.

When I put my empty wineglass on the coffee table, it seemed natural to settle back with my head against Matt's shoulder, just plain nice to have him put his arm around me and stroke my cheek with his fingertips.

Under my ear I could hear the strong beating of his heart, and I smelled his skin—a clean, pleasant scent, like sycamore leaves in the summer sun. I tipped my head, and he kissed me.

An innocent kiss at first, then I felt his hand at my waist, touching my bare skin, slipping up under the sweatshirt. I opened my mouth beneath his and clung tightly. Sweet passion, an easy transition to the couch, ousting the dog, or to the bedroom, except...

There was a sudden hesitation, a mutual wariness.

A hell of a world where you're denied comfort by the fear of sexual contamination and death.

Things got awkward then as we untangled. He offered to give up his bed, to sleep on the couch. No, no, I wouldn't hear of it. He picked up his papers and books, brought out blankets and pillows, turned off the gas log. We said good night.

Leaving the room, he turned back to say "Delilah, it's better this way. One-night stands aren't my style."

"Me neither."

"Rest well."

I did, sleep obliterating thoughts of Harry and Erik. Charlie. Matt…I had a warm body to share my bed after all. During the night, Ozzie jumped up on the couch and curled into the curve of my stomach.

In the morning, Matt was gone when I woke up. He left a note on a hall table and a door key. The note read: *Had to be in court early. Come back any time.*

When I left, I scrawled *Thanks again* on the bottom of the note and left it weighted down with the key, just the way I found it.

EIGHTEEN

On the way to the hospital, I picked up a doughnut and coffee to eat in the car. My dollar plus change. Either I had to line up some work today or go back to waiting tables at Mom's.

Harry had regained consciousness early that morning and had been asking for me. He was asleep now, shrunken and small in the narrow bed. I sat beside him and put my hand on his arm.

He opened his eyes. "Miz West?"

The nurse had cautioned me not to let him talk much. A few questions and he was worn out anyway...was I okay? Had they caught the guy who stabbed him?

The stubby eyelashes fluttered down, and his thin chest wheezed in and out. Any time I felt like I was having it rough all I had to do was come and look at Harry.

I slipped out and went to the office. Time to earn a living. I contacted every company, every attorney I'd worked for over the past two years and took anything they offered, including serving subpoenas. No sumo wrestlers. I drew the line there.

Tomorrow would be a busy day. Meanwhile, I had most of the afternoon left to work on the Collins case.

Rita called as I was getting ready to leave. "Must have been a slow night. You didn't wind up in the headlines this morning."

"It had its moments. What's up?"

She said that Lucy Taylor had tried to reach me once this morning and twice last night. I debated whether to call Lucy back or go see her. Might as well drive over.

The phone rang again as I headed for the door.

"Sorry I missed you this morning," Matt said." I didn't have the heart to wake you up."

"I had a good sleep. I appreciate your taking me in."

"When do you start the new job?"

"I don't. Listen, Matt, I'm going to spend some time today working on Mike's case. I'll call you later and fill you in."

"Why don't we do it over dinner?"

I said okay and promised to leave a message if I missed him. A long time until dinner, so I took the jar of Fisher's unsalted peanuts with me and ate them in the car while I reviewed the suspects.

Even though Warren had an alibi, I hadn't ruled him out. Not with good old Eddie around, that jack of all criminal trades. But connecting the two bothered me.

In the first place, how would somebody like Warren get in touch with a guy like Eddie Anson? But say Warren *had* stumbled across the man, there was still a problem. Eddie didn't strike me as either subtle or clever. And somehow I thought that's what Warren would look for in a hit man.

On the other hand, what if Charlie had been right about Pam Jacobs? She and her daughter got most of the money.

Carolyn—I hated even thinking of her as a suspect, but it was time to stop being ruled by my emotions and start putting together timetables. Thanks to Bill Irwin, I knew where Warren was the night Mr. Collins died. Ken *said* he had been working late. Pam had refused to answer the question. I wondered what the Jacobses' maid would say.

While I looked for a pay phone, I thought of two surefire ways of getting Pam and Carolyn out of the house so I could go over for a chat with Nguyet.

When Nguyet answered, I asked for Mrs. Jacobs.

"Sorry, not at home. Return at three o'clock."

"Is Carolyn in?"

"Not home. Working at mall with Mr. Jacobs."

What can I say? Sometimes you get lucky.

I hightailed it up to Cresta Verde. Lucy would have to wait.

Nguyet opened the door and recognized me. "Not here, nobody here."

She tried to close the door, but I put my weight against it. "I came to talk to you, Nguyet."

"Me?" Her eyes widened with fear. "Why talk to me?"

"I just wanted to ask you a few questions. Please—can I come in? It's chilly standing here."

She shook her head. "No. Missus Jacobs say you not come in. Pliss, you leave now."

"Nguyet, I know Mrs. Jacobs is upset about my investigation. The reason she's upset is that I told her that her father was murdered. That's a very painful thing for her to deal with. So she gets angry and says it couldn't possibly be true. But terrible things happen, Nguyet. Mrs. Jacobs can deny them but they still happen."

I'd struck a chord. She nodded slowly, then stood aside so I could come in.

"Maybe we could have some coffee," I suggested. "Could we do that? Just sit in the kitchen and talk?"

Another nod. She led the way. A Mr. Coffee kept a pot warm on a white-tiled counter. She brought two steaming mugs to a bleached oak table and sat down, eyeing me apprehensively.

I explained that I was trying to reconstruct everybody's movements the night Mr. Collins died. I carefully did not refer to anybody as a suspect. I was sure she understood English a lot better than she spoke it. I thought she understood more than I was telling her too.

"Do you know where Mrs. Jacobs was that evening?" I asked.

"Here."

"She was here all evening? She didn't go out at all?"

"For dinner," she admitted. "But after dinner, here all the time."

"What time did she come home?"

"Not sure. Eight-thirty, nine."

"You saw her?"

"Yes."

"And she didn't go out again?"

A hesitation. Then she shook her head.

"You were working here in the house—doing what, cleaning up?"

"No."

"Where were you?"

"My room," she said.

"Then how do you know Mrs. Jacobs didn't leave again?"

"My room is over garage. I didn't hear car."

"I see." I sipped my coffee. "So you were in your room—were you reading—watching television—"

"Yes," she said. "Watching TV."

"Then maybe she left and you just didn't hear."

She shook her head, but I could see she was considering the possibility.

"Nguyet, I'm sure you have a good job here and you like it—"

"No," she said. "I don't like. In Saigon I was teacher." She lifted her chin and looked at me. "I work very hard now learning English. I will not be a maid always."

"I'm sure you won't."

"I say what I think is true. Missus Jacobs here all night. But to know for certain—" She hesitated. "I cannot say this."

I thought a jury might tend to believe that Pam hadn't left the house. I leaned that way myself. When I asked, Nguyet told me that Carolyn came home from an evening class at nine-thirty. Nguyet didn't think that Carolyn had left again either, but again she couldn't be certain.

We'd finished our coffee. I didn't ask for more, and she didn't offer. She kept glancing at the clock.

I thanked her for talking to me, wished her good luck, and left. It was only two-fifteen, but I was sure she didn't relax until I was safely down the driveway.

On the way to Terrace Towers, I thought about Pam and Carolyn. Alibis didn't let them off the hook, of course. But trying to imagine either of them making a deal with a lowlife like Eddie Anson was even harder than a scenario between Warren and Eddie.

So now I was back to Ken. If he couldn't account for his whereabouts, let's say he had opportunity. How about motive? He must have known it was only a matter of time before Pam asked for a divorce, so he couldn't count on getting a share of Mr. Collins's money.

Back to square one. What I needed was a new flash of intuition, but nothing happened. So I thought about dinner with Matt instead. I'd give him a call as soon as I finished talking with Lucy.

Outside the rain had stopped and the streets were dry, but the sky was sullen, leaden. Two weeks of winter and that was enough. I was ready for spring.

As I drove past Linda Vista Park I noticed somebody had sneaked in between showers and planted a bed of pansies, bright yellow and a deep velvety purple. I found a parking space and walked over to Terrace Towers, cheered up until my thoughts segued back to Mr. Collins.

I wondered if the murderer could still be somebody I hadn't even met yet and remembered Carolyn's contention that her grandfather was unhappy with the hotel. A lot of digging left to do.

Inside, I got a frosty look from Doris Beardsley. I'd lied to her to get the information I needed. Just doing my job. Like Charlie had been doing his. What was the difference? I went over to stand by her desk.

She ignored me, tapping furiously at a computer keyboard. Letters leaped across the amber screen.

"Mrs. Beardsley—"

"I've very busy right now," she said coldly.

"I know you resent the way I handled our interview the other day—"

She stopped typing and looked up. "You lied."

I winced. "Yes, I did. At the time it seemed like the best way to get the information I needed."

"You could've asked me."

"Would you have told me? Or would you've thought those things were none of my business?" I indicated a side chair. "May I sit down?"

She considered. Nodded.

I sat and explained my suspicions about Joe Collins's death. I told her about Mike. "It's easier for the family to believe that Mr. Collins wandered into the street and Mike ran him down. Murder's sordid, ugly."

"But who could've done it?" She leaned forward, fascinated.

"I don't know yet. Maybe you could help me. You gave me names of some of his friends, and I've spoken to Lucy Taylor. What I need to know—was there anybody he didn't get along with? Did he ever argue with anybody—over the poker game, for instance?"

"No." She drew the word out, thinking.

"Maybe over a woman?"

"They do that, you know. People think because you get old you lose interest in sex, but the things I could tell you...Now Joe—I thought for a while he and Lucy—he asked me about her once. Wanted to know all about her, personal stuff. Of course, I told him the files were confidential."

"Did he say why he wanted this information?"

She shook her head. "No, but I knew he was pretty well off. I thought he really was getting interested in her and was being care- ful. But later—well, it was obvious nothing was going on between them."

"Doris," I said. Chummy. Still playing the game. Well, it was my job, dammit. "Doris, I don't know how true this is. It's something Joe's granddaughter said to me. She said he was unhappy, that he'd become dissatisfied with living here at Terrace Towers." I could see her hackles rising, so I added quickly, "No place is perfect, I know that. But if I knew what was bothering him, it might help."

"Well, we have our problems, of course."

"Of course."

"Mostly it's the food. Not enough red meat. You'd think they'd never heard of cholesterol. Or they complain about the staff. We've had to fire a few people because of complaints."

"Anybody recently?"

"One of the housecleaning staff."

I could see she was reluctant to talk about it. "What happened?"

"Some things were missing," she said. "Nothing very expensive. Jewelry, mostly with sentimental value."

"Was this person arrested?"

"No. Mr. Hernandez decided not to call the police. The woman denied taking the things, and both of us believed her. She'd worked here for years, and there really wasn't any proof."

But the woman had lost her job because somebody complained. Joe Collins? Could the motive for his murder really be that simple?

"Doris, who complained?"

"Lucy," she said. "Lucy Taylor."

NINETEEN

Theft...now I had a common denominator. And I also had a thief. Not the cleaning woman. Lucy...

I thanked Doris for helping me and went over to use the house phone. Hesitated. If my suspicions were anywhere near the mark...I headed for the front door.

"Wasn't she in?" Doris asked.

"I forgot something. I'll be back in a second."

I went out to my car and retrieved my gun. Probably a waste of time, but no sense taking chances.

Back inside, Lucy answered on the second ring and told me to come right up.

Of course Lucy must have been the one stealing things here at the hotel. Accusing the cleaning woman—good strategy. Deflect attention, confuse the issue. But somehow, Joe Collins found out...

Lucy threw open the door as soon as I knocked.

"Delilah, hello. You certainly are hard to get hold of. I called you several times."

She wore a misty-blue dress the color of her eyes with touches of lace at the collar. Her white hair curled softly against her pink cheeks. She walked without the cane. I could see it leaning against a dinette chair.

"Your leg's better," I said.

"Yes, it is, thank goodness. Come and sit down while I make us some tea."

She bustled around. Would I like Earl Grey? A little early for sherry, but if I'd prefer that—

"Tea's fine." I hung my coat on a wall hook by the door and went to sit on the big chair positioned at a right angle to the sofa. I wedged my purse beside me. The hard outline of the Smith and Wesson pressed against my thigh. *Probably* not necessary, still…

She started the teakettle, got down cups and saucers, put them on a tray, added a sugar bowl. "The list is there on the end table, Delilah."

"List?"

"You know, the people who were at the Greenspace meeting the night Joe died."

I picked it up. Handwritten names on a sheet of yellow lined paper. Beautiful penmanship. Each name was followed by a check mark: blue, red, or green.

"I tried to think of everybody who ever attended a meeting," she said. "Then I called to see if they went that night."

The check marks were a code. Blue if they'd attended, red if they hadn't, green if she couldn't get hold of them to ask.

"Great." And where were you, Lucy? Were you really home nursing your ankle?

"You do think it will help?" She watched me, eyes bright behind the wire-rimmed glasses.

I pretended to study the names. "Let's hope so. Thanks."

"Well, if there's anything else—I do want to help—"

The kettle whistled and she busied herself, making the tea, putting cookies on a plate. The picture of grandmotherly charm. Could she possibly be a murderer? She'd been pretty desperate when I recognized her. So afraid I'd turn her in to the cops.

What if Mr. Collins threatened to have her arrested? Would she have killed him over that? The way Doris described the thefts made them sound like pretty small potatoes. Lucy could've made restitution, maybe talked her way out of it. But there had been another robbery, the one at the jewelry store—

"Delilah? Sugar or lemon?" She put the tray on the coffee table and sat on the sofa.

"Just plain, please."

I remembered tracking her that day in South Coast Plaza, how expertly she'd slipped things into her bag. No question that she had been at the mall to steal. Had she nipped on over from May Company to Jacobs for a real heist?

"Delilah?" She held out a steaming cup, waiting.

I took it.

She picked up hers, took a sugar cube with a pair of tongs, and dropped it in. Stirred. I'd bet the tongs were sterling silver. From May Company?

"Is something wrong, dear? You seem awfully preoccupied."

"Just a little tired."

"You do look worn out. You must be working too hard. Have you made any progress at all?"

"A little." I sipped the tea. "I identified Eddie Anson for the police."

Her cup clattered against the saucer. "Who?"

"The man who attacked me and stabbed Harry Polk." His rap sheet had said that he was, among other things, a fence. Lucy was a thief, and thieves need somebody to fence the things they steal.

She put down her cup and wiped her fingertips on an embroidered napkin. "You found out his name."

"Didn't I tell you? I picked out his mug shot."

"No—no, you didn't. I suppose the police put out an—what is it?—an A.P.—?"

"An A.P.B. Yes."

If I was waiting for her to quiver and shake and start babbling her guilt, it wasn't happening. Instead she beamed me a hundred-watt smile and declared, "Why, that's *wonderful*. I think you must have a real knack for this private eye business. Have a cookie, dear. I confess I didn't bake them myself, but they are good, and I'm sure you can use the energy."

I eyed the thick, nut-studded goodies. If she really was a murderer, this seemed like a real good time for her to get rid of me. She'd drunk from the same pot of tea, but—a little spritz of arsenic on the Pepperidge Farm…

She took the top cookie and nibbled on it, held out the plate.

I took one, feeling a little silly. Was this whole scenario just another wild leap to a conclusion based on circumstantial evidence? I'd been so sure Amy Ferguson was the killer, and Erik and Charlie were covering it up. That mistake still smarted. And it made me leery of following my own judgment, encouraging me to stay and poke around some more.

I bit into the cookie. White chocolate and macadamia nut. "The night Joe died—you told me he was supposed to come and see you."

"Yes, that's right. But he never showed up."

"Didn't you think that was strange? Weren't you worried about him?"

"No, not really. I thought the meeting ran late, or he got side-tracked. It wasn't exactly a *date*, you know, although—Delilah, can I tell you something?"

I gave an encouraging nod.

"Joe and I—we really were getting close, very close, and I even hoped—that we—"

Her face crumpled and her hands shook, sloshing tea all over the front of her dress. She put down the cup, jumped up, and dabbed at herself with the napkin. "Oh, dear, such a mess, excuse me—" She rushed off toward her bedroom.

I put down my own cup. And the cookie. A nice old lady breaking down over the death of a friend—why did I have this sudden rash of goose flesh icing my neck?

No tears, that was why.

I slid open the zipper of my purse. Just in case she came out of the other room with a pistol of her own or a bread knife. Or there was always the cane. She could make a detour, pick it up—the bedroom door opened and Lucy came back, patting her eyes with a big wad of Kleenex.

"I'm so sorry, Delilah, giving way like that."

She came over and sat down on the sofa. If she had a weapon, she'd done a damn good job of concealing it.

"I don't care if it is early," she said. "I really do need some sherry. Would you mind pouring me some, dear?"

I kept an eye on her while I went into the kitchen, took the liquor and a glass from the cupboard. She wiped her eyes again, but I'd bet money that tissue was dry.

Okay—so—I'd give her the sherry and then no more cat-and-mousing around. I'd beat it out of here. Share my suspicions with Brady—well, maybe not Brady. With Matt or Charlie. Get Charlie to check her out. Who knows—maybe she had a record. Hell, maybe she did a few ax murders on the side.

I poured her sherry and took it over. Fingerprints—did Charlie have some way of plugging into the Cal I.D. computer system and running fingerprints? Lucy's should be on the list she'd made up. What if they weren't? I glanced at the coffee table. She'd handled the sugar tongs. If I could swipe those—just to be sure—

I saw her move—quick as a snake—knew she wasn't just reaching for the glass as light glinted on the thing in her hand, and knew there was no time to react. She grabbed my wrist. I dropped the sherry, tried to yank away. Felt the sting of a needle in my upper arm, my right arm.

With the left, I lashed out at her. I twisted and pulled. Her glasses flew off but she held on, tucking her head down, and pushed the plunger on the syringe. Something hot raced up my arm.

"God *damn* it—"

I swung and connected.

She slumped back in the chair and I stumbled away. The needle was still in my arm. I yanked it out. Blood bubbled.

"What is it? Wha' did you—" My voice thickened.

Two of her now—four fox eyes—gleaming. Door—get to—door. I tried, but my knees buckled. Not a thing I could do as the floor rose up to hit me in the face.

My office floor—Jesus, I was sick of it—like sleeping on a rock pile. Bad dreams. A nightmare, a real screamer. Hypos and passing out—

I lay very still, afraid to open my eyes. Not the smooth nylon of my sleeping bag against my cheek. A rug. And that smell…the dark, rich odor of spilled sherry.

Lucy…

My arms were behind my back, bound with adhesive tape. I could feel it, sticking and pulling. I flexed my ankles slightly, enough so I could tell they were bound too. A small effort, but it started a whirlpool in my head, dark and thundering. I tried not to move at all, terrified of being swept under.

Was she here, watching? *What the hell did you give me, you crazy old bitch?*

Maybe she'd gone. Just wanted a head start, like that day in the mall. The drug would wear off and I'd drag myself to the door, yell until somebody came.

I strained to hear some sound that would give me a clue. I lay on my side, one ear pressed against the floor—big help that was. Anyway, if she was still there, best to play possum. Let the whirlpool subside.

My eyelids itched with the effort to stay closed. My breathing grew ragged.

Shit.

I peeked out from beneath my lashes.

She sat on the sofa, three feet away, watching me. Wearing her glasses so she had no problem seeing. She pressed an ice bag against her cheek.

My purse was gone from the chair. I'd been so cautious, going back to the car for the .38. Then I'd let my guard down…

"Delilah?" she said.

I closed my eyes. A creak from the sofa. Rustles, clinks from the coffee table. The squish of her feet on the carpet.

I opened my eyes the narrowest slit. Through my eyelashes I could see her kneeling beside me.

"Delilah?"

I tensed. Noise and surprise, that's all I had left. I opened my mouth and pushed my shoulder up and back, trying for fast forward but all I got was slo-mo. My scream for help was only a squeaky yelp, then the black eddy swirled, almost sucked me under.

When the world stopped spinning, I groaned. The sound was muffled and the movement hurt my lips. Then I understood what she was doing when she got up from the sofa. Cutting a piece of adhesive tape. And she'd come over and slapped it across my mouth.

I looked up. She was coming back from the kitchen with another glass of sherry.

"I *thought* you were awake." She lifted the glass in a little salute and drank. "You just never give up, do you? Well, of course that's the problem, isn't it?"

She brought her glass over and sat back down on the sofa. I could see her cheek was puffy and discolored. She took a swallow, then put the sherry on the coffee table and picked up something. I couldn't see what it was.

"Not very nice of you, Delilah, hitting an old lady. I'm going to have a nasty bruise."

"Mfmftt—" I said. Something like that.

She held up a hypodermic syringe and a small vial. "I had to guess at the dosage to give you before and I guessed wrong." She jabbed the needle through the cork in the vial and withdrew the solution.

I felt hollow and cold. If she thought she'd get that stuff into me without a fight…

Somebody knocked on the door, three soft raps. Yelling was out but I thrashed around and banged my feet on the floor.

"Oh, for heaven's sake." Lucy put down the needle and stood up. "It's only Eddie." Her eyes gleaming merrily. "You remember Eddie, don't you, Delilah?"

TWENTY

Eddie Anson glared down at me and summed up his feelings succinctly. "This is a buncha shit. What the fuck you think I am, Lucy? A garbageman?"

He was certainly dressed for it. Through slitted eyes, I saw filthy jeans, a T-shirt that had probably been white sometime in the dim past, a dirty frayed denim jacket, boots with run-over heels, the leather so scuffed they looked like they'd been worked over with a razor blade. I had a good view of the boots from my vantage point on the floor.

"If you'd done your job right the first time," Lucy snapped, "we wouldn't be in this mess."

"Me?" He sounded indignant, a little hurt.

"Dumping Joe in the street like that. What a dumb stunt that was."

"Well, it woulda worked. If it wasn't for *her*—"

I'd stared into the eyes of a shark one time at SeaWorld. Eddie's eyes looked like that, completely lightless, dead dark holes. There was a fresh pink scar running diagonally across his face. I sincerely hoped I'd put it there.

"Oh, yes," Lucy said, "and you really took care of that problem. 'Don't worry about it, Lucy. I'm gonna make sure she butts out, Lucy.' You ever pay attention to those bloodthirsty movies you go to? You ever notice how criminals wear a ski mask? Or a stocking over their faces?"

"Yeah, so?"

"She made you, you stupid ass," Lucy said. "She I.D.'d you to the cops."

"Christ!" His eyes lit now with a savage, surface shine. "Knew I shoulda wasted her. She fuckin' cut my *face*—"

He drew back a scuffed boot, aiming for my head, but I rolled away and he connected with my shoulder blade. Pain jolted through my body, but it had a funny once-removed feeling. At least the dope in my system was good for something.

"Eddie," Lucy said sharply. "Stop fooling around. We have to make some plans."

"I got plans. Oh, fuck yeah, I got *big* plans—"

"Later. Right now—" She picked up the hypo.

"What's that for?" he asked.

"We've got things to do and I don't want to have to worry about our friend here."

She told him to hold me down, and he was happy to help out. A sting in my arm and the whirlpool started, sucking me down into its great black maw...

Voices...a long way off. I was in a deep pit. A long, exhausting climb up. So, hell with it. Better to lie low anyway. Down here, no need to worry about needles or hard-toed boots.

"...going to do it, do it right..."

"...fuckin' easy for you to say..."

Lucy and Eddie. Wonderful pair. Made for each other.

"...have to do it anyway, so let's get it over and done with." Lucy, the mastermind, planning something—something to do with me?

Better start paying attention. I tried, I really did, but as soon as I exerted a little effort...

Blackness...

A phrase here and there.

*When you...the mall...*mumble, mumble, *fuckin' CRAZY...two million retail...back door...*more mumbles...*automatic spritzers...*

Spritzers?

Well, see, she really had doctored up these cookies and I ate one and keeled over—no, wrong, not the cookies. She'd stuck a needle in my arm and...

I drifted back.

The room was quiet. Somehow I knew Eddie had left. Maybe they'd both gone. Oh, sure, fat chance. A cautious peek and I could see Lucy. She sat on the couch with a big ball of fluffy pink yarn in her lap, knitting. I swear she was.

Reaction, I guess. I just couldn't help it. My eyes flew open.

Lucy glanced over. "Awake already? I guess I still don't have the dosage right." She caught my incredulous glance at her needlework. "Keeps my fingers in shape. Arthritis, you know. I'm not nearly as good at my work as I used to be."

Her work. I didn't for a minute think she meant knitting.

"Oh, I do keep my hand in," she said. "Sometimes I just can't help myself. Like here at the hotel. You'd be surprised what you can find, Delilah. Jewelry, of course. Money. But we have two doctors here and a veterinarian. They keep all kinds of interesting medications and, of course, everybody has hypodermic syringes. I used to have them myself when my husband was alive. Howard had diabetes. Poor dear, just couldn't give himself the shots so I had to do it. But listen to me, rattling on." Her needles flew faster. My own personal Madame Defarge.

This was bad. This was terrible. She was an *old lady*, for Chrissake, and she'd got the best of me not once, but twice now.

I moved—I think I had the crazy idea of standing up—but my body felt like it could be poured into a Jell-O mold.

"Not feeling too well, dear?" Lucy inquired sweetly. "Your own fault, you know. If you weren't so nosy—and persistent—"

My stomach churned. I tried to tell her, but the adhesive tape over my mouth reduced everything to a hopeless gargle.

"What's that, dear?" she said.

I had the feeling she guessed what I was trying to say. I also thought she'd probably sit there and watch me drown in my own vomit.

I will not throw up, I vowed.

"You're probably wishing I'd give you another shot," she said. "Well…I could do it. I still might. But Eddie would be very upset. He's got these special plans that he wants you wide awake for."

Plans. Of course. She didn't intend for me to lie around and become a permanent part of the decor. I dimly remembered bits and pieces of their conversation. Not good, I knew that, even though I couldn't recall details.

What the hell had she done with my purse? If I could get my hands on my gun…trussed up like a turkey, this was not exactly a viable possibility.

Think, for God's sake.

Eddie had left the apartment—to do what? Get his boots shined? Have his teeth cleaned? No, now I remembered. He'd gone shopping.

Uh-huh. Sure. For a new outfit, no doubt. What the best-dressed man wears to off a nosy P.I.

"Delilah?" Lucy said.

I closed my eyes, hoping she'd get the hint and shut up. A buzzsaw worked on the back of my head so it was hard enough to concentrate.

She sighed, and I heard the knitting needles click.

Let's see. Where was I?

Eddie had left the apartment. Where had he gone?

Shopping, my mind promptly supplied. Shopping at the mall. *Eddie?* Well, that's what I'd heard. Eddie had gone to the mall.

When? How long ago?

I had no way of knowing. No feeling for how much time had passed. But the lights were on in the apartment, and I was sure it was dark outside.

Dinner with Matt was definitely off. And breakfast. And probably any future we might have had together. Would he worry that

I didn't telephone? Suspect something was wrong? Call out the National Guard? No, I was the tough lady P.I. No reason to worry about me.

I wished to hell I could remember what Eddie and Lucy had been talking about so I could anticipate their plans, at least. I might not have registered everything the two of them had said, but surely, on some subconscious level, the gist of the conversation was there. They were going to get rid of me. That was a given. But, dammit, what else?

While I racked my brain, I flexed my wrists, hoping to find some slack in the adhesive tape, but I might as well have been bound with heavy-gauge wire. My mouth was slightly open beneath the gag so I began pushing at the tape with my tongue and curling my lips.

Whatever Eddie was doing, he was doing it at the mall. South Coast Plaza? Another bit of their conversation popped into my head. *Two million retail*...Ken Jacobs might have that much in inventory. Had she sent Eddie off to burglarize the jewelry store?

The couch creaked. Footsteps. Water ran in the kitchen sink. More footsteps. I peered out from behind my eyelashes. She was getting antsy. Pacing around, looking at her watch.

Enough hypothesizing. Whatever Eddie was doing, I had the feeling she expected him back soon. And I knew damn well what was next on the agenda when he arrived.

I pushed frantically at the gag with my tongue. A long way from coming loose. Too long. I tasted glue and my jaws ached. Maybe if I made enough noise, attracted some attention...I eased over on my back, bent my knees, and began drumming on the floor as hard as I could.

"Good *heavens*," Lucy said, startled.

Sweat popped out on my forehead. I was parallel to the coffee table. If I could get myself swung around and give it a good kick before the top of my skull came off—better still if I could give Lucy a good kick...

She stood out of reach and shook her head with a smile. "That won't do a bit of good, you know. Grace Wong lives down below me, and she's deaf as a post."

I had turned just enough. I gave the coffee table a good solid bash. A cup went flying. A glass. Her knitting.

"That's *enough*," she said. She went over and picked up her cane.

I remembered the autopsy on Joe Collins. *Massive cerebral hemorrhage.* I'd bet there were traces of blood on that carved wood handle.

I stopped kicking the table. My strength had all run out anyway. I breathed in short, erratic gasps, not getting nearly enough air through my nostrils to fill my lungs.

"That's better," Lucy said.

Through the roaring in my ears I heard a knock on the door.

"Well, it's about time," Lucy said, and went to let Eddie in.

TWENTY-ONE

"Jesus, what happened here?" Eddie asked, eyeing me and the overturned coffee table.

"Delilah had a little temper tantrum," Lucy said.

"Yeah? Well, maybe she oughta be cooled off a little." Eddie clearly relished the prospect.

"No, leave her alone. I don't want somebody to see you carrying her down to the car like a sack of potatoes. You'll be a good girl, won't you, Delilah?"

I looked at Eddie's boots. Defiance was not in order, so I inclined my head in a nod.

"I thought you'd be sensible." Lucy turned to Eddie. "Pick up that table for me. What happened at the mall? Is everything under control?"

He righted the table. "Yeah, great. Piece of cake."

I could hear the false heartiness in his voice. So did Lucy.

"What happened?" she demanded. "Something went wrong, didn't it?"

"Nothing much. The kid walked in. I had to slap her around a little, that's all."

The kid. Carolyn. *Not home*, Nguyet had said. *Working at mall with Mr. Jacobs.*

"But you handled it?"

"Fuckin' A. Listen, you got anything to eat in this place? I'm starvin'."

"You want to eat *now*? Oh well, it might be better to wait a few more minutes anyway. Make sure everybody's asleep."

The dishes I'd kicked off the table were still on the floor. She picked them up, giving me a severe glance. "Now, you be nice, Delilah. No more noise or I'll let Eddie deal with you."

If noise was going to help me, there would have been some response by now. Nobody had heard me, or maybe nobody wanted to make a fuss. I had to get out of here. Not just for myself anymore. *I had to slap her around*...what had he done to Carolyn? And Ken—what about Ken Jacobs? He would never stand by and see his daughter hurt, so Eddie must have "handled" Ken too.

Out in the kitchen, the refrigerator opened and closed. Dishes clattered. I caught a whiff of mustard, the oily spice of bologna.

Well, now I knew what the two of them had been planning and where Eddie had gone. I even knew what time it was—approximately. Eddie had gone to the mall, all right, but not to go shopping. He'd hung around, waited for closing time, and robbed the jewelry store.

Jacobs closed at nine; say an hour to wrap up things, a half hour to drive back here. That meant it was between ten-thirty and eleven o'clock.

Oh, you're some detective, I told myself.

"You're sure nothing else went wrong?" Lucy finally sounded nervous.

"I told you—you got any cheese? Swiss, that's good—I went in right when he was getting ready to lock the door. He says, 'I'm closing now.' And I say, 'You go right ahead. I just came for a little talk.' Then I showed him the knife—how about mayo? Jesus, how can you eat a sandwich without mayo?"

I looked around desperately. I might be able to roll over to the door. I might even be able to get there before they saw me. But standing up and turning the deadbolt—good luck.

Face it. My only option might be to wait. If Lucy didn't want Eddie to carry me out slung over his shoulder, he'd have to untape my feet. Maybe sometime on the way out, there'd be an opening.

Somebody, please God, might be out for a walk or coming back from dinner or a movie. Any kind of distraction and I'd make a break.

But did I dare count on any of this?

I could feel time slipping by and I kept remembering Eddie's knife going into Harry's stomach. Had Eddie used the knife on Ken and Carolyn?

"What I don't understand," Lucy was saying, "is how the girl got into the middle of things."

"She came in the back way. She went out for fuckin' pizza. What's the big deal? I told you everything's cool."

Lucy hadn't bothered to pick up her knitting. Eddie had set one leg of the table in the middle of the tangled pink skein. One of the knitting needles was gone, but the other one was there, anchored by the rows of stitches. If I could get to that needle...

I rolled over toward it.

In the kitchen, Eddie was opening the refrigerator again. "Diet pop? Is that all you got?"

"So drink water," Lucy snapped.

They came out, Eddie carrying a plate and a pop can. I froze. The lamp on the end table beside the sofa shone like a damned spotlight. If they glanced my way...

They went over to the small dinette table. I took a shaky breath. The sofa served as a room divider; now it also provided a screen. When they sat down, I couldn't see them. Therefore, thank God, they couldn't see me.

"What about the rest of it?" Lucy said. "Did you stop at Target?"

"Didn't have to. Ol' Ken had everything we need right there in the back room."

Closer to the coffee table now, I could see the other knitting needle. There was about half an inch clearance between the flap of material along the bottom of the sofa and the carpet. With my view at floor level, I could see that the needle had slid under the sofa. Something else was under there too. A small pair of scissors, the kind used for needlework. Too bad my purse was nowhere around.

"I don't know about this two-million shit." I couldn't see Eddie, but I could tell he was talking with his mouth full. "He ain't got much stock over there."

"Quality, Eddie, not quantity. What he has got is the best."

Another roll and my nose was an inch away from the soft wool. This was the tricky part. I was lying facing the coffee table and the sofa, so I had to alternately pull with my shoulder and push with my heels to scoot my body up and around the coffee table, ending up with my back against the sofa.

I shoved off. There was just a whisper of my clothes sliding against the carpet pile but with so little room to maneuver...I bumped the end table. The lamp swayed and my heart hammered.

I leaned against the table to steady it. The lamp kept jiggling. Dammit, *dammit*...If either of them looked this way...

The lamp settled back in place.

I lay for a second, listening to see if they'd heard anything, letting my heartbeat slow down.

"Just one thing, Eddie," Lucy said. "I hope you didn't get some bright idea about helping yourself to a little bonus over there."

"Would I do that?"

A rhetorical question, I presumed.

"You'd better not have because I'm going to check the inventory sheets."

"Jesus! That's a nice way to talk. We're partners, remember?"

"I haven't forgotten that," Lucy said coldly. "I just hope you didn't."

Almost there. I sweated with the effort, and my muscles quivered. A brief rest leaning against the soft upholstery. Just a few more inches and I'd know if the scissors were close enough for the restricted reach of my fingers.

Don't even think about it. They had to be.

I hope you didn't help yourself to a little bonus.

What was that all about? Eddie had gone to Jacobs to rob the place, hadn't he? And why was Lucy talking about checking inventory sheets?

My fingers touched the scissors. Never mind figuring out Eddie and Lucy's schemes. Cutting myself loose required all my concentration.

The tight wrapping of adhesive had cut off some of the circulation, so my fingers were clumsy as I pulled the blades apart and maneuvered one of them between my wrists. The sharp point dug into my skin, sending a new sliver of pain up my arm.

Once I had the blades in place, I tried grasping the loops of the handle so I could get a scissoring, cutting action. No way. Too awkward.

"Will you hurry up?" Lucy was saying.

"What's the rush? They ain't going anywhere."

"I'll feel better when it's over with and you're on that plane."

I spread the scissor handles and pushed the V of the blades against the tape, using it like a knife. I could feel the slack immediately. Two seconds and one side was done.

I rotated my right wrist, pulling, ripping all the fine hairs loose from the adhesive. It hurt like hell, but the worst thing was I couldn't turn my hand enough to get loose. I would have to cut the other side of the tape.

I fumbled the scissors back in place.

Dishes clanked and a chair scraped on the tile. Tidying up...and then they'd go out to the kitchen and...

My hands were freer now so I could hold the scissor handles and take a big fast snip. One more and the tape parted. Quickly I clipped one side of the tape wound around my ankles.

"I still think you're silly," Lucy said. "Taking those stones with you. I've got contacts. I can get a lot more for you."

"Oh, yeah, right. Just leave 'em all here. You'd like that, wouldn't you, so you could—" He stood up, saw me, yelled, "Hey!"

Hastily I angled the scissors down to cut the other side of the tape on my ankles, jabbing a long bloody slash in my skin.

"Fuckin' *bitch*." Eddie came around the sofa. Lucy was behind him.

I was still on the floor between the sofa and the coffee table. I jerked the scissors up.

"Watch out," Lucy cried.

He saw them too, hesitated. "Oh, you're cute. You're real fuckin' cute."

I yanked the tape off my mouth, wincing. Then, keeping the scissors ready to feint, I pushed against the sofa to lever myself up. My legs felt shaky. A trill of pain crawled along my shoulder, reminding me that Eddie had been using me for a soccer ball.

"You're dead," Eddie said. "Oh yeah, you are."

The knife. Where was his knife? No outline of it on his body. In his boot?

"I gave you one scar, Eddie." I stepped backward, working my way along the couch. "This time I'm going for your eye."

"Do something," Lucy said. "Don't just stand there."

But he didn't close in. "Get my jacket."

"What are you talking about?" Lucy said.

"Get my fuckin' *jacket*," he snarled.

So now I knew where his knife was. He'd left his coat slung on one of the dinette chairs. Lucy scurried for it.

Once he had the knife…I risked a quick glance around. Where the bloody *hell* was my purse? Screw it. Could I take him with the small scissors? Too risky. I made a break for the front door. Swearing, he dived after me, staying low as he grabbed me.

I got in one good jab. Not his eye, unfortunately. He bellowed as the scissors gouged a chunk of flesh from his biceps. His hand closed on my wrist. He twisted and shook the scissors loose. I felt ligaments tear. I clawed at his face with my free hand.

Eddie, with his usual finesse, simply belted me with his fist and sent me sprawling. Then he was on top of me, hands knotted in my hair, banging my head on the floor.

"Stop it," Lucy cried. "Stop it, Eddie. Cut it out."

"Gonna fuckin' *kill* her—"

"Later. For God's sake, the noise, Eddie. Somebody'll call the cops."

He finally listened to her. My ears rang and sparklers danced in my head. Eddie sat astride me, his fingers still tangled in my hair. I could feel his hands shaking and could smell his sweat mixed with the brassy scent of the blood running down his arm.

"I'm gonna do her right now," Eddie said.

His eyes popped with excitement. A man who really enjoyed his work.

"Not here," Lucy snapped. "A mess like that. Forget it. Now calm down. We're going to do things the way we planned."

"I don't like it."

"You don't have to like it. Tie her back up. You'll just have to carry her down."

They had a brief but heated discussion on what to use. Seems Eddie had left the roll of adhesive tape at Jacobs. If he'd used it on Ken and Carolyn, maybe they were still alive.

And if I husbanded the little bit of strength I had left, sometime on the way downstairs or out in the street, maybe I could still get away.

And maybe pigs will fly.

"Well, find something," Eddie said. "Jesus. We'll be here all fuckin' night."

"I don't expect to have to tie people up," Lucy said tartly. "It's not like I have ropes lying around—" Struck by a thought, she smiled. "Wait a second."

She went to rummage around in the kitchen and came back with an extension cord. Eddie's lips peeled back in a big grin.

"Oh, yeah," he said, and looped the cord around my neck.

A savage twist cut off my supply of air.

I made gagging sounds as I clawed feebly at his hands. Another twist. A red mist filled my head to bursting.

Eddie released the cord a little, still grinning as I choked and coughed.

"Well, okay," he said, delighted. "That's more like it."

TWENTY-TWO

They took me down a fire escape. The extension cord noose was so effective Eddie didn't even bother tying me up. It didn't matter anyway. We passed nobody in the hall.

I had one forlorn hope that someone had heard all the racket and called 911. I imagined a squad car speeding silently down the street, slamming to a stop, cops spilling out, *Hold it right there, asshole!*

But the only traffic was an Audi and then a Buick cruising by, the occupants caught up in their own little worlds behind the fishbowl of windshields.

Eddie marched me along like a lassoed steer. Lucy trailed behind. She'd put on a fleece coat and had a big leather purse slung over her shoulder. Eddie stopped beside a gold Cadillac and fished in his pocket for the keys.

"What are you doing?" Lucy said. "This is Ken's car."

"Whadduya think, I'm gonna drive my old junker when I can go in style?"

He dragged me around to the back of the car and opened the trunk. "Get in."

When I hesitated, he started twisting the cord around my neck. I climbed up. There are inside releases in trunks. Flares, maybe. Jack handles.

He went to work. Quick and sloppy but he got the job done. I lay on my side with my knees under my chin. One end of the extension cord stayed around my neck. The other went down my back to wind around my wrists and then my ankles. He pulled the cord taut. No slack at all. Any movement tightened the noose.

He slammed the lid, and I lay in total darkness.

The manhandling sent pain shooting up from my wrist, arrowing out in all directions. I moved cautiously and felt that awful, strangling pressure at my throat. It didn't make any difference what was in the trunk—Ken could've stored a M60 back there and I wouldn't be able to use it.

At least it was a smooth ride. I thanked God for the Caddy's padded trunk liner, and—as Eddie hit a chuck hole—for heavy-duty shocks. If only it were warmer. They hadn't bothered with my coat, and I shivered in the chill blackness.

Where were they taking me? I tried to keep up with the turns, but by the time I could feel the big car accelerating and knew we were on the freeway, I had no idea which direction we were headed. Were they going to dump me in the desert? Off a pier into the Pacific? Maybe just in a ravine off Ortega Highway in the local mountains— that was another favorite of local murderers.

Why hadn't I taken a minute to call Matt and tell him my suspicions about Lucy? Because I'd been afraid that I'd look like an idiot if I was wrong, that's why. I certainly hadn't been scared, me with my Smith and Wesson. And I'd kept rationalizing right down to the last. Lucy seemed so *nice*.

Yeah, Ma Barker had probably been a sweet old lady too.

The only consolation I had was that my actions hadn't caused Ken and Carolyn's predicament. Lucy and Eddie had already planned the robbery. I'd just stumbled in at the wrong time.

I had a feeling I still didn't know the whole story, but I could piece together a few things. Lucy had been stealing at Terrace Towers. I was pretty sure she'd also taken the things from Ken's shop. She'd admitted killing Joe Collins.

How much had he known? He lived in the hotel and might have seen something to make him suspicious of Lucy, but it was a hell of a jump to connect her with the original robbery at the jewelry store. I hadn't made the connection, and I knew firsthand about Lucy's light-fingered habits.

Whatever Joe knew, she killed him for it—or damned near killed him—then called Eddie to dispose of the body. Eddie—lazy Eddie—had a flash of genius and left Joe in the street. I suppose he figured even if nobody actually ran over the old guy, it still might look like a hit and run. Actually he would've lucked out if I hadn't come along.

Lucy must've been chewing nails, especially when I recognized her. No wonder she sicced Eddie on me.

The car slowed and turned. An exit ramp, I thought. But exit to where? I hoped we arrived damn quick. The air in the trunk felt thick and smelled of rubber. Pretty soon I'd be gasping like a landed fish. If I lost consciousness and pulled on the cord, I could strangle myself. Save Eddie the job.

More stop and go, more turns. Then they came to a halt and shut off the engine. I lay there waiting. Now I'd know what they were going to do with me. Unless they were planning to leave me in the trunk. Walk away. Call somebody to pick them up. Call a cab.

A metallic *skritch* as the key turned in the lock and then the trunk sprang open. I drew a long shuddering breath.

"I see you're still here." Eddie grinned down at me.

His skin and teeth looked yellow. We were in a parking lot lit with sodium vapor lights. A building loomed on one side, and I thought it looked familiar. Freeway traffic hummed nearby.

Eddie worked on the knots tying my ankles, yanking on the noose, deliberately, I'm sure. I choked and coughed.

"Hurry up," Lucy ordered. "You want the patrol to see us?"

She stood by the car looking around, pulling on a pair of thin, black leather gloves.

My feet were free. Eddie yanked me out of the trunk. He left my hands tied, attached to the noose. A blast of icy wind hit me, and I shivered some more.

"Cold?" Eddie asked. "Well, you're gonna be plenty warm soon enough."

He laughed and nudged me ahead of him, holding the extension cord like a leash. I knew where we were now. South Coast Plaza. A wing of the mall jutted out on the left. An entrance over there, but it would be locked. Not our destination anyway.

Mall shops have back doors for deliveries. The layout was simple. Rear entrances were grouped around large alcoves. Each alcove has a pull-down, garage-type door, locked of course. We headed for one of the alcoves, and Eddie produced a key ring, unlocked the door, pushed it up with a chattering creak of pulleys and gears, then pulled it down behind us.

In the dim light I could see white letters stenciled on a line of gray doors. A barred gate had been added across the one marked *Jacobs*. Eddie opened the gate and the inner door.

He flipped a light switch, and the three of us trooped in. We were in the small room in back of Ken Jacobs's jewelry store. Carolyn was on the floor, her hands and feet taped, tape over her mouth. More tape attached her to a straight metal chair. She'd tipped the chair over. I thought she'd been trying to reach her father.

Ken lay facedown on a cot, bound hand and foot too. Which meant he was alive when Eddie left him. You don't tie up a dead man. I wasn't sure Ken was still alive. His skin looked pasty gray, and he wasn't moving. Blood soaked his left sleeve. More on his back. A big stain on the cot beneath him.

Carolyn looked at me, eyes huge with terror in her pale face. A bruise discolored her jaw, and there was blood on the tape that covered her mouth.

" 'S all right." The words came out a croak. I was surprised I could talk at all.

"Oh, yeah, things are fuckin' wonderful." Eddie poked Carolyn with a booted toe. "Ain't that right?"

"Knock it off," Lucy said sharply. "Let's get finished here." She tilted her head, scanning the ceiling. "You sure you took care of everything?"

"Told you I did."

I followed her gaze, looking up.

Automatic spritzers. My insides turned icy. No, what Eddie had said was *sprinklers.* Somebody—Eddie, it had to be Eddie—had worked over the nozzled heads. A crude job but the pipe looked crimped enough so water wouldn't flow.

Jesus…

Did you stop at Target?

Didn't have to. Ol' Ken had everything we need…

You're gonna be plenty warm soon enough.

A clutter of boxes in the room. The ones Ken had been packing in his garage. One was ripped open. The one marked Solvents on the outside with a black marker. I knew what was in it. Paint remover. Lacquer thinner. Oily rags.

I looked back at Carolyn. Knowledge jumped between us. Either Eddie had told her his plans or she'd figured it out too.

There would be an alarm system. Had Eddie been smart enough to disable that too? Probably not, but what difference did it make? This room would be an inferno long before the fire department arrived.

"All right," Lucy said, satisfied. "Give me the keys and you stay here with them."

"No fuckin' way," Eddie growled.

"Honor among thieves," I said. "You're a real pair."

"Shut her up," Lucy ordered.

Eddie did, quite effectively.

He headed for the showroom door, dragging me along. Lucy followed. A dim light burned in the shop. Through the windows I could see out into the big empty mall. Not fully lighted but a lot brighter than the shop. A clock above the counter glowed faintly: 12:05.

Security guards checked the huge mall every hour, one to each floor, covering their beats in electric golf carts. How long since the last sweep?

Lucy took a penlight from her purse along with a padded mailer. Eddie unlocked the sliding panels at the back of the display cases, and Lucy began cleaning them out, putting the jewelry in the mailer.

Eddie never took his eyes off her.

"You'd better be watching for security," Lucy said, "instead of worrying about me stiffing you."

The language no longer sounded strange coming from the little old lady. As a matter of fact, she didn't look so sweet anymore. Her face had a lupine set. The wolf in grandmother's bed letting its nightcap slip off so you got a look at the cruel eyes and sharp teeth.

I glanced back out at the mall. Where was the damned patrol? During my stint at May Company, I'd had a routine security briefing and met the staff. Part of the briefing had been a handout detailing the guards' schedule. I'd only scanned the material; there'd been no need to commit it to memory.

Lucy scooped up the last of the jewelry and put the mailer back in her purse. She watched the mall too. "All right. Let's go." She headed for the back room. We followed.

Think about the patrols logically. The mall was laid out like a big H, with the security offices located in the middle, in that connecting bar. Leaving the offices, the guards would have to make two circuits to cover the end sections. A half hour for each section—but which half hour for this end of the mall? And what was the starting time?

I held back, frantically scanning the enormous corridors for any sign of movement, until Eddie shoved me through the door and closed it behind us.

Now, even if the patrol did come by, he wouldn't see anything unusual—until the whole shop was aflame, and by then it would be too late.

TWENTY-THREE

Eddie shoved me down on the floor. I guess he figured he didn't have to worry about permanency. He simply anchored me by lifting the cot and slipping one of its legs between my back and the stretch of extension cord linking my neck to my hands.

Then he went over to the box of solvents, took out two of the flat metal cans, and opened them. One in each hand, he splashed the liquid on the stack of boxes. Lacquer thinner. The sharp odor stung my nose.

Carolyn made high-pitched squeals behind the tape and wriggled against the chair, her eyes glazed with helpless terror. On the cot above me Ken groaned.

Eddie poured some of the stuff on Carolyn's dress. More on the cot. My eyes burned from the fumes. He grinned down at me.

"The cops are going to get you, Eddie," I said hoarsely. "Or they'll get Lucy and she'll make a deal."

He kept grinning, a sardonic lift at one corner of the mouth, a look that said, I may be dumb but I ain't stupid 'cause, baby, I got *plans*.

"Will you get a move on?" Lucy stood by the back door, radiating a jittery excitement.

He opened more cans and tipped them over on the floor. "That oughta do it."

I thought I could get loose from the cot. I was sure I could. Push my body up under the bedframe, a quick heave, then while the leg was off the floor, slide the cord under and out. Like skipping rope. All in the timing.

Eddie slipped his hand in his jacket and took out the switch-blade. He knew I saw it. A secret, crafty gleam in his eyes.

Now. I had to make my move now before he came at me. I brought up my knee for leverage, tensed my shoulders.

Eddie turned away and walked toward the exit.

Then it hit me.

His back had been turned so Lucy hadn't seen him take out the switchblade. And he was holding the knife so it was hidden.

"Lucy," I shouted. "Look out."

Not that I cared if and when Eddie stabbed her. I just wanted both of them occupied so I could make like Houdini.

His surprise blown, Eddie brought up the knife, flicked out the blade.

"Oh, Eddie," Lucy said. "You pathetic ass."

Push. Heave. Twist. I slipped free from the cot.

"Sorry, Granny—" Eddie took a step toward Lucy, and she shot him.

The gunshot boomed like thunder in the little room. My ears rang. Eddie took another step. Just reflex. Then he dropped like a poled steer.

I stayed where I was, taking it all in. Poor Eddie. Like me, he'd underestimated Lucy. She'd had a gun in her purse all along. There was a big hole in it now. She hadn't bothered to remove the gun, but had just shot him through the leather bag.

She took the gun out, and I recognized it. My trusty Smith and Wesson.

Plenty of stopping power. It stopped Eddie all right. Noisy too. If the guard was anywhere in this section of the mall, he might have heard the shot.

Playing it safe, Lucy kept my .38 ready as she went over to Eddie.

"I guess I should thank you for warning me, Delilah." She prodded Eddie's body with the toe of her shoe.

I lay still. Did she know I'd gotten loose from the cot?

"Thank me by walking away from here," I said. "Nobody'll find us till morning. You can catch a flight, be out of the country by then."

"I wish I could. But I do hate flying, dear. And I really don't want to spend the rest of my life in a foreign country. I'm too old to adjust."

Satisfied that Eddie was out of commission, she knelt beside him, the movement stiff and awkward. She was only a few feet away from me. Hell, everything in the room was only a few feet away.

My mouth was dry and my heart pounded. She thought I was safely out of the way, otherwise she'd never have gotten down on her knees beside Eddie. Although she exploited the fact that she was an old lady, she knew her limitations.

She searched Eddie's pockets, the ones closest to her. Keys, of course. She needed the keys to the door and the car.

Moving slowly, I eased up on my knees too. I kept my back against the cot leg, hoping she'd think I was still connected to it.

She swung the gun up. "Stay still. Stop moving around."

"Okay. All right."

She went back to her search. Eddie was right-handed. The keys would be in his other pocket.

She would have to reach across his body and turn slightly away. She hesitated.

Do it...

She leaned over him.

I launched myself at her, using my head for a battering ram. Hit her square in the midriff. She grunted and her breath rushed from her lungs. But not the best move for me. One blow too many and the room went out of focus, hazed with that damned red mist. Like the special effects in a bad movie.

I shook my head. Precious seconds, then the fog cleared. I was back on my knees. She'd fallen on Eddie. Now she was trying to stand up, holding her chest. Breathing though. A hoarse honking whoop.

The gun—where was the damn gun? On the floor at her feet. We both saw it.

No contest.

She reached for it, but I jumped to my feet and kicked it away.

She looked up at me. Still doubled over, holding her chest. I knew what I had to do.

But I hesitated.

Yes, I knew she was a thief and a murderer and that she planned to toss a match into the room on her way out and burn me and Carolyn and Ken up alive. That she would still do it.

But, dammit, she was an old lady—old and weak and—at that moment—vulnerable.

So I hesitated—for about two seconds.

Then I kicked her twice, as hard as I could, once snapping an ankle and again, aiming for the center of that sweet, soft chin.

TWENTY-FOUR

Different hospital, but for the second time that week I was back in an emergency room. So were Carolyn and Ken. And Lucy too. After being triaged, so I lay in a curtained cubicle and waited while they stabilized Ken, then treated Lucy.

To be perfectly honest, I was delighted to be lying in a nice clean bed, even a hospital bed. I just wished somebody would give me an aspirin. I hurt all over. Wrists, arms, shoulders. Either my brain was expanding or my skull was collapsing. And the way my foot throbbed, I was sure I'd broken a toe.

One consolation—in addition to a fractured ankle, Lucy had a broken jaw and a cracked vertebra in her neck.

When the admissions clerk came around with her little clipboard and asked about my insurance, I told her I worked for Erik Lundstrom. I'd come clean tomorrow and check myself out, but tonight I wasn't about to go back to my office.

The clerk asked if there was anybody she could call for me.

Rita? Jorge? Hoa? Matt…

One kiss and one night on his couch did not make a lifetime commitment.

I told her there was nobody.

After they patched me up, Lieutenant Brady wanted a preliminary statement. The doctor ordered Brady to keep it short. I gave him the abridged version.

"Let's get this straight," Brady said. "You *kicked* an old lady like that?"

"You're damned right. That old lady was about to turn us into Crispy Critters."

He bought the story; he had to with Carolyn to verify it, but he was still a little revolted.

After he left, Carolyn and Pam came in for a minute. An aide was getting ready to take me to a room. Still no aspirin. They'd given me a shot instead. Nothing like the stuff Lucy pumped into me, but at least it took the edge off the pain.

"Are you okay?" Carolyn showed her lumps, but she looked pretty good.

"Fine," I said. "How's your dad?"

"He's in surgery. He's lost so much blood—I knew the bleeding was bad. All the time I was lying there, I could see him—but I couldn't *help* him—" Her voice broke.

"It's not your fault," Pam said. "Baby, you did the best you could. Didn't she, Miss West?"

"You sure did," I told Carolyn. "You tried. That's what counts."

"But look what they did to you, and you got us out of it."

"Oh, that." I tried a grin. "Just luck."

"I don't think so," Pam said. "I owe you an apology, Miss West."

"Delilah."

"Delilah. God knows how I'll ever thank you—"

"You just did."

The aide said firmly that it was time for me to go up to my room. I agreed completely.

I wanted to tell Carolyn that her father was going to be all right, but I knew she didn't want false hope. So I just said, "One thing I hope you learned tonight, kiddo. It's never over till it's over."

I thought I was going to get a good night's sleep.

Wrong.

Nurses kept whispering in and out, shining lights in my eyes. When I did sleep I dreamed. I was back in the jewelry shop. I'd only imagined Lucy shooting Eddie. They went out the back door, and Eddie tossed in a match.

I dreamed I was in the ambulance with Harry, sirens wailing.

I dreamed that Erik sat beside my bed, brushing my hair away from my face. I heard him say "Shh, sleep now. You're safe."

I also thought I'd feel better the next morning.

Another mistake.

I still had a king-size headache, and every time I moved, I found new and unusual places that hurt. Ken Jacobs had made it through surgery and the prognosis was good. Lucy, while in terrible pain, was being sweet and brave and had convinced the staff that she'd somehow wandered into the middle of things, poor dear.

When a clerk brought in the paperwork for me to sign, I tried to 'fess up about my job, but she kept insisting that everything was covered. I figured I'd argue the point later when my headache subsided.

Just then I had people lined up to see me. Lieutenant Brady was first in line, of course. But I'd made the papers again. The nurse said dryly that for somebody who claimed to have no friends, there were an awful lot of strangers crowded into the waiting room.

Rita and Farley. Jorge and Consuelo. Hoa. A few more people from Mom's. Arlene Simpson.

Matt.

He waited for the rest of them to clear out and came and stood beside the bed.

"I thought you stood me up last night," he said.

"Sorry."

"If I knew you a little better, maybe I'd've been worried instead of just pissed off. Jesus, it scares me to think—" He sat down and grabbed my hands, holding them tightly while he told me the wheels were in motion and Mike would be out soon.

An aide arrived with a wheelchair to escort me out of the hospital.

"Do you have a place to go?" Matt asked. "Because if you don't—"

Rita stuck her head in to say Farley was waiting downstairs with the car.

"I guess you're set then," Matt said. "Call me?"

"Don't worry. You still owe me a dinner, remember?"

And—just maybe—breakfast too.

When I arrived at Rita's, Charlie called, muttered a few sheepish apologies, then added, "I tapped a few police sources and thought you might be interested in what I found out. Ken Jacobs was making regular payments, ten thousand a crack, to—guess who?"

"Lucy?"

"Right. I got curious this morning and ran a background check on her. This old gal's a real pro, Delilah. She and her husband had a standard scam. They'd steal some jewelry, wait for the owner to collect the insurance, then approach him, offer to sell back the ice, cut rate, and suggest that the transaction could be kept quiet so the shop owner could pocket the profit from the insurance payoff. If he bit—bingo. Blackmail express."

And Ken fell for it.

In a few days I got the rest of the story. Lucy hadn't pulled the blackmail scam since her husband died, but Ken had been too perfect a mark to pass up. She'd heard all about his business troubles from Joe Collins. What she hadn't planned on was how quickly Ken would fold. He'd gone to Joe, told him about Lucy, and Joe threatened to turn her over to the police.

After I told Ken that Joe might have been murdered, Ken began to suspect Lucy. No wonder he was shaky. He said he never actually told Lucy about his suspicions, but I'll bet she guessed.

Lucy didn't admit to any of this, of course. She was back doing her grandma shtick, in the Orange County Jail awaiting trial, knitting booties for all the jail staff's new arrivals.

While Ken recovered from his stab wounds, Pam visited almost every day, and when he was indicted for insurance fraud, she put up bail and hired a sharp defense lawyer who promptly got Ken off on a technicality.

As for Warren, he received a slap on the wrist from the EPA, but the newspapers wouldn't let the story die. Penn Industries sold the division to a corporate raider who used it for a tax write-off and dismantled the company. Warren's currently selling refrigerators at Sears while he looks for a new management position.

Carolyn got it into her head that the family owed Mike Morales an apology. They met for coffee, then for a pizza. Now they spend all their free time together. Pam's frantic and blames me.

Harry recovered and is back on the job. Both jobs. Building custodian and self-appointed assistant private eye. There's a lot for him to do these days. I've had a stampede of new clients and enough money coming in so I rented a condo and paid off Rita.

Matt and I have had dinner several times, and—once—breakfast.

The rain stopped in February. We've had nothing but glorious sunshine ever since and predictions of a drought.

I made another attempt to settle with the hospital for my stay, but they said the bill had already been paid—anonymously. Erik…I think maybe he really was in my room that night. I'm also sure he's partially responsible for my prosperity. I have my pride but—hey— why be stupid and turn away business?

Anyway, no sense being modest. I do the work and do it well. I'm a pretty good detective.

Hold it.

Scratch that.

I'm *damn* good.

At least that's what Matt tells me.

ABOUT THE AUTHOR

MAXINE O'CALLAGHAN was born in Tennessee in 1937 and grew up in the boot heel of Missouri as a sharecropper's child. She was the first in her large extended family to finish high school and left a few days after graduation with ten dollars and a bus ticket for Memphis. She went from there to Miami where she joined the Marine Corp Reserve and then to Chicago where she went on active duty for a while and got her first taste of California during basic training at the Recruit Depot in San Diego.

In 1972 she moved with her husband and two children to Orange County, CA, a long way from the cotton fields of her childhood. As a stay-at-home mom, she began her writing career with short stories, including one in *Alfred Hitchcock's Mystery Magazine* about a private detective named Delilah West, which predates both Marcia Muller and Sue Grafton's entry into the female PI genre. She published thirteen novels and a collection of short stories. She has been nominated for both the Anthony and Bram Stoker award. Her novels and short fiction featuring Delilah West were honored by the Private Eye Writers of America with their lifetime achievement award, The Eye, for her contribution to the field.

40181196R00108

Made in the USA
Charleston, SC
26 March 2015